LET THE WOODS KEEP OUR BODIES

E. M. ROY

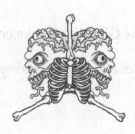

Ghoulish Books
an imprint of Perpetual Motion Machine Publishing
San Antonio, Texas

Let the Woods Keep Our Bodies
Copyright © 2023 E. M. Roy

ISBN: 978-1-943720-89-7

www.GhoulishBooks.com

Cover by Ryan Caskey

For Mum, Dad, and my sibling.

AFTER

THERE WAS NEVER a terror upon this town. The most trouble folks could get into was limited to speeding tickets and neighborly squabbles that ended with all parties involved getting brunch the next day and laughing over drinks. Cops spent every morning in the town's sole Dunkin' Donuts, just like on TV, with too-sweet coffee between them and good-natured hellos to the residents they knew—pretty much all of them—who also came in every morning. It's really no surprise. With an overall population of less than eight-thousand people, good old Eston gave the impression that the few folks who stuck around after high school weren't the type to cause real problems. Things simply didn't happen here. The tragic events worldwide which so often pervaded the news were far away and alien. For a lot of people, this made it hard to care. It's not affecting them, it would never happen in Eston, so best not invest energy in bringing the conflict to their front doors. Too much of a hassle. It was an unspoken agreement that quietness was a virtue. Quiet was safe. Eston was safe. No crime, no conflict, no one ever got hurt or killed.

The newfound tremor in Leo Bates' hands felt utterly out of place.

It was the first time in days that it wasn't raining for hours on end, and Leo was thankful. The rain would soon turn to snow, probably within the next month, and she wasn't quite prepared for yet another winter in Maine. The nervous tic she had developed would only be compounded by the cold.

Time was passing in a way that left Leo disjointed. How long had it been? Two days at the most . . . right? Or had it been weeks, months? She paused mid-stride to snatch her phone out of the back pocket of her jeans, its luminescent screen standing out painfully against the dark and wet pavement below. Friday, eighth of September. Exactly four months after her own eighteenth birthday, and exactly three days after Tate Mulder went missing. Three days. An ache shot from temple to temple, and after a moment, she returned the phone to her pocket and picked up her pace.

The girl found herself glancing over her shoulder more than once as she left the school's vacant campus. "This town is about as secure as you can get," her aunt would repeat to her several times a day after the incident with Tate. The reassurance always came with a disdainful up-and-down glance at Leo. "Ask anyone. Nothing will hurt you." Leo believed her. To convince herself, she waved a silent greeting to the older couple who lived in the small blue house across the street from the high school, and they each smiled back from their chairs, their graying Labrador rising to his paws with swollen joints which Leo could almost hear creaking like rusted hinges. However much she would have liked to pet the old dog as she so often did before, she hoped he wouldn't waste his energy bounding up to greet her. She wanted to get home and off the streets.

The old couple and their dog were a tranquil sight. Always sitting out on their little flaking porch in paint-chipped chairs, the dog resting at their feet. Watching the kids walk home from school, or more recently, watching the traffic bottleneck onto the main road. When Leo pictured the trio, she could visualize their aging like a timelapse; surely three years ago when she was a freshman they hadn't all been so grizzled, but she supposed they might as well have been. She never knew a time when that dog was in any fashion resembling a puppy. Even when she attended the middle school just a few blocks down the street. The consoling, familiar sight of them had the ability to soften the cruelest of traumas. Almost. *Nothing will hurt me.*

Most days, she could contain the trembling to certain parts of her body. It would simmer there for a while until she was distracted enough to forget it. This was a rare occurrence, if she's being fair. *A sort of nausea about the hands;* the corners of Leo's mouth twitched into a smile, vaporized breath escaping into the too-early September chill like the ghost of a laugh. Sartre was one of the select authors in English class whose words found a way to echo around her head for weeks after a lesson. Not due to any sort of scholarly awe, but because of the man's pretentiousness and how goddamn depressing the book *Nausea* was to the point where Leo needed to ridicule it to let it occupy space in her mind at all. It was stupid—she recalled herself and Tate encountering minor inconveniences and lamenting with the phrase *"My HAND!"* on a near-daily basis, and despite the repetition, it always got a big laugh between them—but there was a weight to Sartre's words now that wiped the grin from her face. Nausea started in her hands. *Tate.* Then it gorged itself on her organs. A tightening which took root in her stomach and then climbed up her ribs like a grotesque ladder as if threatening to collapse her chest with each heaved breath. It culminated in a headache that fed itself off the audible beat of her heart. It was an infinite feedback loop attempting to fill a void. The fear was auto-cannibalistic. This was not happening now, during Leo's solitary walk home, but almost certainly would later that night. She shoved her hands in her coat pockets.

Lucky that she didn't live too far from the school. Hardly anyone was out walking, especially not kids. The past two—sorry, *three*—days had resulted in an undeclared curfew of sorts. Except it was only about three o'clock in the afternoon. Things didn't happen here. *So when something did, people didn't want to talk about it, huh? Turned a blind eye. Except not so blind that you let your kids go out alone.* Nevertheless, she kept walking, turning out onto the sidewalk of the main road. Her aunt and uncle let her out, anyway. That was proof in itself that everything was fine.

No sooner had she faced the oncoming traffic from the sidewalk did Leo spot a police car parked on the shoulder down the street. It was easy to speed down this road, so this was a common sight, if not for the cop being so intentionally and visibly positioned. Like it was waiting for something.

Leo had only ever been approached by a cop once. This past summer had been full of drives over unpaved roads and the busier town center. She had never been a huge fan of driving just to drive, but Tate was. They usually went to the Eston Public Library (which Leo had quite possibly never set foot within pre-Tate) or parked in an empty parking lot with a pair of iced coffees and stolen cigarettes. Nothing too bad.

"Wanna go for a drive?" The question was posed whenever the weather was neither blistering nor chilled. A rarer occurrence than you'd think. Maine dealt in absolutes; you got burnt to a crisp, or you lost a toe to frostbite. There was no in between. Leo would rather lose a toe.

An overdramatic sigh to match an exasperated response. "I *guess,* if you *insist,* god, you're—"

"A great friend who loves spending time with you, I know!" Tate finished with a wide grin which Leo couldn't help but mirror after a time. Leo took the driver's seat, and Tate's sole responsibility was to choose the soundtrack for their journey—a most distinguished honor in Leo's car. Tate played lots of indie stuff, the trendy kind. Leo didn't complain, but she did slip some grunge beats into the rotation every once in a while.

As much as she found it strange to admit in the

beginning, these drives became coveted events that Leo eagerly awaited. Time spent alone with Tate in such a temporary and in-between space felt both calming and thrilling. They barely knew each other, had just started talking at the start of the summer. And that was only after Tate had made a concerted effort to interact with the avoidant Leo. She would sometimes catch Tate staring at her from across the school cafeteria or the hallway and, at the time, simply chalked it down to a morbid curiosity. Or pity. Leo possessed quite a reputation, to be fair. All the same, it felt as though the two girls had known each other for eons and yet had secrets they were still unwilling to share.

The unlikely pair would either sing along to an old jam (Tate needing to nudge Leo to join in her unabashed belting, to which Leo eventually gave in) or, more often, engage in conversations that didn't seem to fit in any immobile space. They were constantly moving, leaving one conversation behind and picking up another on the way. When neither girl was in this space, the topics died. Leo didn't have to make eye contact, as she was the one driving. This made it easier. The drives were ephemeral and catalysts for confession.

"Leo," Tate said after a stretch of silence as they'd pulled up to a stoplight.

"Hmm?" She chanced a look to the girl beside her, the newborn summer lingering in the air between them as a quiet reassurance, before the light turned green and she looked straight ahead again to advance with a blush.

"How did you know you were gay?"

She froze and the blush turned extreme. "Uh. I mean. I just," Leo said. No one had ever asked her that question. Knuckles turned white on the steering wheel. Her aunt and uncle had been accepting enough; the latter surprised and the former a bit dismayed at first. It became an issue that Leo tried her best to avoid at home. God forbid if one of them were to ever ask about girls or relationships.

"Sorry," Tate rushed. Leo felt that Tate was mirroring her own forward stare, not daring to look at her. "That was a weird question."

"No, it wasn't." Leo steeled herself. "I figured it out when I was a kid. All the other girls in school would talk about boys they liked. And I just felt—indifferent," she said. "Or jealous." A bead of sweat dripped down her sternum.

When Tate was quiet, Leo flicked her gaze to the passenger's seat. Wild curls obscured much of her profile, but Leo could see that she was biting her lip. Tate met her eyes, and Leo quickly locked hers back on the road.

"Yeah," Tate said with a breath. "I've been figuring some stuff out, too."

"Oh?"

"Maybe you know already, I dunno." She hoped that she did.

"What?"

"I think it's pretty obvious." It wasn't.

"That you're . . . "

"Bisexual." Oh. Oh! Leo felt like she was flying. Or falling.

Abruptly, Tate leaned forward and looked in the rearview mirror. "Oh, shit," she said.

Driving on complete autopilot with her heart thudding and mind racing, Leo realized too late that she was going 60 in a 45. A cop flashed its red and blue lights with a whine of its siren, the colors bouncing off of Tate's face and widened eyes. Leo's first speeding ticket, and first time ever being pulled over in general, had happened at perhaps the worst moment possible. It was the best $130 she'd ever had to pay.

The two remembered this conversation often in the following weeks of the summer, laughing in earnest at every retelling. It had opened the door to a summer of love and obsession, which would always be destined to end with an ache.

Now Leo continued to walk along her daily route home, which was obstructed by the cop car lying in wait for its prey on the shoulder of the road. Slow steps, one foot in front of the other, while gripping the straps of her backpack. Just don't look; it's not here for you. Leo swallowed and studied her battered knockoff Doc Martens. The fake leather was starting to crack and peel off. Unheedful of her avoidance, the car revved to life and crawled up beside her, crunching gravel beneath its tires.

"Leonora Bates?" The cop, a heavyset middle-aged man she did not recognize, leaned over the passenger seat to ask through the open window.

"Yes?" She squinted to discern his expression, which seemed to be deliberately hidden behind dark sunglasses and thick facial hair.

"I'm gonna need you to come with me, dear," he grunted, stepping out to open the back seats. Leo would've felt more afraid if his "dear" hadn't come out as more of a throaty New England "dee-yah" with an added note of condescension. She tucked the longer wisps of reddish hair which had escaped the disheveled bun behind her ear.

"What's this about?" Leo demanded more steadily than she expected. Of course, though, she already knew. Her fair brows knitted themselves into an oft-worn scowl.

"The disappearance of Tate Mulder. We got some questions we'd like to ask you. I'll have my guys call your aunt and uncle, let 'em know where you're at."

She held his gaze. "My aunt Deb talked to you guys a few days ago."

"I'm aware of that, dear, but some new evidence came up that we'd like your own thoughts on. Please don't argue and just come with me to the station." The man held the back door open and gestured for her to step inside. Cars and trucks whizzed by a mere few feet from where they were standing, intermittent rushes of wind distorting some of his words. Leo thought he attempted a smile, but it lost its way behind his scruffiness and came out as more of a grimace.

Best to be quiet. Best to go along with it. Eston is safe. She got in the car without another word.

BEFORE

"**HEY**," **CALLED A** voice from the road. Leo was sitting cross-legged in her family's petite but overgrown yard. Sebago, the old German shepherd mutt, lay against her thigh and chewed a withered toy she'd been throwing for her. It was imperative to find any excuse to get out of the house during the first weeks of summer, even if she was only a few steps out the front door. Both Leo and the dog looked up to see a figure standing at the top of their driveway. Backlit by the sun, they were an undefined silhouette.

Tate Mulder stepped forward, with her signature dazzling smile and a hand raised in a wave.

"Uh. Hi?" Leo said with a squint through the summer sun. Tate Mulder was one of the most well-liked girls in their class, often one to eat lunch with people who sat alone in the cafeteria or console someone crying in the bathroom. Leo admired this about the girl, of course—she would be an asshole if she didn't—but she also didn't trust it. There were no such things as pure intentions. She was certain that Tate logged all of those charitable acts with gold stars on her long list of elite out-of-state college applications. Which is precisely why she'd avoided her at all costs at school. Whatever Tate wanted from her now, whatever dumb community service project she was recruiting for to uphold her image as angel of Eston, Leo wasn't in the least bit interested.

Sebago stood up and let out a deep woof, tail wagging.

Leo shushed her, but before she could grab her collar, the dog trotted up to Tate with a slobbery chew toy hooked on one tooth and staring up at her expectantly.

"Oh, baby *girl!* What's your name?" Tate cooed at the dog as she knelt to scratch the top of her head.

"That's Sebago," Leo answered. Sebago dropped her toy, which Tate picked up and jogged over to Leo with. The dog came bounding behind, gait all lopsided and goofy with joy at a newcomer's presence. Some guard dog.

"Aw, Sebago! She's adorable," Tate said. Leo picked at a few strands of grass. There was a pause, and her visitor cringed slightly. "Uh. I'm Tate."

"I know," Leo said. She shuffled, face warm. How could she *not* know who this girl was? She held her hand over her eyes so she didn't have to peer through the light. "I'm Leo."

"I know." Tate's shoulders relaxed. "I live, like, just down the road. Didn't we take the same bus in middle school?" Her grin widened. "I swear you wore the same shirt every day for like two months back in sixth grade. What was on it? Something about aliens. It was funny."

"Listen, we all had an alien phase," Leo protested in surprise. In fact, the shirt in question depicted a xenomorph from 1979's *Alien,* worn almost every single day with diligent enthusiasm after Leo had been fixated on the character of Ellen Ripley for weeks. The shirt was now tucked away at the bottom of Leo's closet with the shame of an abandoned obsession. Some boy had made fun of her for wearing it so often, so there it would stay banished forevermore. Sebago tugged at the toy in Tate's hand, which she threw across the yard for the dog to sprint after.

"Aliens are cool. But honestly, I'm more of a Bigfoot kinda gal."

Leo blinked. "Bigfoot, huh?"

"Oh, hell yeah. Imagine being just some dude who lives in the woods, gets to pose for one picture, and then becomes one of the most famous urban legends in history. Iconic."

"I suppose that *is* the ideal life," Leo conceded with a flat tone that she hoped would give her visitor the cue to take her leave. *So why are you in my driveway, exactly?* She bit her tongue.

Sebago head-butted Leo in the shoulder with a huff. "So high maintenance, Sebbie," she said under her breath, chucking Sebago's toy as far as she could into the woods just beyond her house. The dog lunged into the underbrush giddily.

"She's so sweet," Tate said after her, bending down to sit with Leo in the grass. Leo's nerves prickled. "Think I know where she gets it from." Tate winked.

Leo glared. "There's nothing sweet about me," she said, then bit back a self-inflicted curse. Stupid.

"That right? I think you act like you aren't. But there's a sweetheart in there somewhere. You should let her out more often. Happy would look good on you."

Damningly charming and insufferable. But Tate's warm-toned eyes glinted with plain honesty, not in the least pitying. Matter-of-fact. Leo had to avert her gaze. "Who says I'm not perfectly content the way I am?"

She chuckled at that. Tate leaned back with her hands on the grass. "How about the bags under your eyes? Or the fact that I've never, not once in my life, seen you with a real, genuine smile? Like, I mean a *big* one. A real grin that lights up your face. The most I've seen from you is that little twitch that could either be the tiniest smirk on earth or a sign that you're having a stroke. I can't tell."

"That's the *worst*, you know. Telling someone to smile more. Especially when it comes from someone you barely know." Leo's eyes flashed, and now she *really* wished Tate would leave. "But hey, maybe I will. I'll smile bigger and bigger until my eight rows of dagger-teeth are exposed, and my mouth stretches back to my ears, and I'll unhinge my jaw to consume you whole like an eldritch beast. Like a Lovecraftian wet dream."

Tate raised her eyebrows, and just for a moment, Leo

thought she'd succeeded in weirding her out. But then Tate met her eyes with a devious glint. She spoke with the tone of someone who had come to an unexpected discovery. "Oh, I like you." This, of course, prompted a startled full-body blush from Leo, much to her displeasure. If Tate noticed this, she said nothing and shrugged, brushing away a handful of her unruly black curls that fell into her face as she did so. "Didn't mean any offense. I guess I just think that if you let someone in, you'd be a lot happier, weirdo."

She considered Tate and sat up a little straighter. What was Tate doing, talking to Leo like this? Their knowledge of each other began and ended with the obligatory impersonal greeting as they passed in the school hallway. The discomfort wove a crease between Leo's brows. Let's test her genuineness, then. "Who would I let in?"

Tate smirked. "That's up to you, Bates." Composed, confident, and . . . deliberate. Leo was completely disarmed and parted her lips in search of an appropriate snarky response.

A throaty, ferocious bark sounded from the woods and shattered the tension between Leo and Tate like a pane of glass. Sebbie rarely barked like that for a mutt of her size. Tate stood up immediately. "Is she okay?" she asked. "That sounded—" A round of snarls broke from the scuffling of dead leaves, then a sharp *yip* like a wounded puppy.

Before she was conscious of her actions, Leo was sprinting full-force to the woods. Her sneakers pounded the ground like an irregular pulse. "Sebbie? Sebago, come!" She leaped over a line of bushes and into the sparse trees at the woods' edge, stumbling over twigs. More growls and barks erupted from no discernible direction in Leo's frenzy. *"Come!* Sebbie, here!" The leaves crunched, disturbed under her feet as Leo whirled around in circles and called after the dog. Panic began to wrap a pair of deadly fists around her lungs.

"Leo, over here." It was Tate's voice, smoothed over by a strange calmness that jerked her out of fright. She hadn't seen Tate come after her, but as she bolted over to the source of the sound as best as she could locate it, there she found Tate crouched with Sebago panting at her feet.

She was struck with the sight as she came upon a small clearing. Tate and the dog were positioned in such a way, with the sunlight breaking through the leaves above them, that they looked like figures in a painting. Tate's hand was draped over Sebago's flank with languid care. The dark of her skin was able to stand out from the total black portion of the dog's pelt. Her face was unreadable and half-masked by her dangling curls. Like brush strokes against the dullness of the woods beyond. A study of solace with underlying disquiet.

Leo took a dizzying deep breath and collapsed to her knees across from Tate so that the dog lay between them. "Sebbie, are you okay, baby?" She stroked the dog's side gently as it rose and fell in quick succession. Sebago whined and licked Leo's leg without getting up, and Leo saw that she was shaking. "What was she doing? Did you see?"

Tate was silent. Her stare was focused on Sebago with an intensity that Leo had never seen before. The image of her as a painting was morphed into a three-dimensional fixation that Leo didn't understand. " . . . Tate?"

She flinched and looked up at Leo. "I don't know," Tate said. "Let's just get her out of here before whatever it was comes back."

Leo ended up having to carry the weakened dog back inside her house, arms aching with the weight and face completely buried in Sebago's dark fur. She relied on Tate to guide her with a reassuring hand on Sebago's head as the dog rested her trembling chin on Leo's shoulder.

Her aunt and uncle guessed that poor old Sebbie had a run-in with a skunk or a fisher. Lucky she didn't get sprayed, they said. The dog had a few shallow scratches on her front legs and seemed to be favoring her right hind paw, but had nothing else to show for the scuffle besides a full-body tremor that lasted for hours afterward. No use bringing her to the vet and paying a shitload over a few scratches. Leo had to bite down the urge to argue with her guardians for a vet visit. But she supposed the dog would be okay. Leo treated the wounds and bandaged them with a tenderness that warranted her to speak only in whispers as Tate sat by her side. The quiet company was oddly welcome. Tate's care for Leo's dog caused an ache she couldn't quite place.

"Did you see what it was, Tate?" Leo later asked again, Sebago falling asleep on her pillow in the living room. Leo and Tate each sat on the floor beside the dog's bed, beneath the biggest window. Neither wanted to leave until Sebbie was asleep or, at the very least, had stopped shaking. Whenever one got up, the dog would raise her head and utter a soft whine that broke Leo's heart. Her eyelids were finally beginning to get heavy, though, blinks lasting longer and longer.

Tate shook her head, seemingly not in answer but in sympathy for Sebbie as she pet the dog's velvety ears. The dimmed late light in the living room cast shadows over Tate's face that made it hard to read her expression. They hadn't bothered to turn on the house lights yet, as the setting sun granted them a golden warmth that dappled over Sebbie's fur and the two girls' bodies, giving everything in the room a fiery tinge. Peacefully, they let it burn.

Tate's demeanor had changed since they had found Sebago in the woods. It unnerved Leo in a way that drowned out any trivial suspicion she'd had of the girl before. She leaned in, fixated on the way the almost-orange sunlight outlined Tate's crooked nose—*I wonder if she's broken it before*—and the light riding the wave of her eyelashes. Leo blinked. Stop this. "Talk to me," she said with unexpected force.

Tate glanced at her, then sighed. "Weird things happen sometimes, I guess."

That was the most information she could get out of Tate concerning the event, despite the question being asked repeatedly weeks after the fact. Even after Leo let Tate in, and even after they had begun their strange summer together. The last golden rays faded to darkness, and Leo turned on the lights.

AFTER

SHE SHUFFLED IN the backseat of the police car, fiddling with the hem of her oversized green flannel. She suddenly regretted wearing anything so comfortable on an afternoon which promised to be so unforgiving. It felt inappropriate. She didn't want comfort. Her stomach churned as she remembered this was one of the shirts which Tate most often liked to steal from her. If it was big on Leo to begin with, it fit Tate perfectly, flattering the curve of her hips as if it were made to her exact specifications. Leo took it off to reveal some indecipherable band tee and cast the flannel aside with her thicker coat.

"Too warm back there?" the cop asked, turning down the heat politely as they drove down through the center of town. It was quite a treacherous series of intersections that seemed rather out of place for such a small area. Easily the busiest part of town, with two *whole* bunches of stoplights, if you can imagine that.

"No, it's fine," she mumbled, gaze fixed instead on the approaching expanse of field littered with gravestones. She was freezing. The cemetery was right up ahead. When she was a kid, the stones seemed to stretch away into oblivion. Once in elementary school Leo had attended a field trip to the grounds and had raced gleefully between the headstones, all skinned elbows and half-buttoned overalls, blind to the solemnity of the place. She shuddered. Now she could see that the stones staggered over a shallow ridge and disappeared once the faraway forest loomed up behind

19

them. Before this summer, Leo had never been far enough into the grounds to get a good look at the woods and see just how far they extended—from the road they appeared shadowed and dreary, sure, but still altogether flat. Up close, though, the trees could swallow you whole. Discouraged curious souls from wandering inside, she supposed. The blanket of bulging interwoven clouds overhead certainly didn't help with that. The rain from earlier in the week would likely make an apologetic return later in the day. After all, every graveyard worth its grit needs a good thundershower. Helps to keep the living things moving and the dead things drowned.

If small town cemeteries are used only as obligatory homages to history, then Eston was beating its residents and visitors over the head with the past. The one recognizable landmark in Eston's possession to an outsider was the turnpike exit. Had the name of the town and everything on the sign. Take exit 63 off the interstate and you were in for a treat. As it happens, right across the street, as you got off the turnpike and crossed the threshold of the town center, was the cemetery. Welcome, welcome! Here's all our deceased! Enjoy your stay! Or, more likely, safe travels as you drive straight through on your way to somewhere far more important. The cemetery's prominent placement seemed to be the undead's proclamation of both welcoming and warding off visitors. Conveniently located both in the middle of town and just off the interstate, it was unavoidable. Leo figured most of the headstones were decades upon decades old. But despite this, it was more than plausible that each one still had copious descendants living within a short drive of their resting site. It was likely that she was made from at least one of the forgotten skeletons beneath that ground. Besides the obvious ones.

There's something sinister about it. Placing a relatively busy turnpike exit across from a cemetery. She rarely saw anyone on its grounds, but at the moment, the darkened figure of a girl was sitting cross-legged in front of a grave several rows in, her back facing the road. Leo wished her well.

"You know anyone buried there?" the cop wondered aloud with a clear of his throat, noticing Leo's fixation as they stopped at one of the lights. As she watched, the girl in the cemetery stood up.

"I don't."

"No? Not your parents?"

Leo whipped around to meet his sunglasses in the rearview mirror, cut up from the grate between the front and back seats of the cruiser. "Why do you care?" She almost growled. Then, guessing his expression and to subdue the forewarnings of her temperament that he would inevitably give to his colleagues at the station, she forced her voice into a level of indifference. "Yes, they're buried there."

"Ah, I thought you were Ava's kid." The cop nodded, not convinced of her nonchalance. "How long ago was that now? 'Bout six years? I remember being there. Terrible what happened to 'em—"

"I'd rather not talk about it, if that's okay," Leo blurted. *Eight years, actually*. She could feel his veiled gaze measuring her response in the mirror. "Just not relevant right now," she clarified.

"Everything's relevant right now, dear." *Dee-yah*. Leo's skin prickled.

"What do you mean?"

The man scratched the back of his neck. Leo realized he hadn't given her his name. "Tragedies beget tragedies, is all. You get to noticing that in this line of work," he sighed. At Leo's expression, he continued. "We're just lookin' at everything right now. Can't tell you much here. Wait until the station."

The first warning rumbles of thunder sounded from above them. Rain soon. A chill ran up Leo's spine. She suddenly felt very ill. Why did she need to be questioned again? She had already explained her last encounter with Tate to the police a couple of days ago, just hours after she had vanished. Her official statement had been a solid account of that evening, everything she thought they would've needed to know. *He said they'd found more evidence* . . . What else was there to find? Evidence proving what? She picked at a loose seam in her jeans. Most everyone in Eston seemed to believe (or chose to believe because any other explanation was too horrible to consider) that Tate had simply run away. A story could be strung together to support this. Tate often talked about leaving Eston. They both did. But Leo had also overheard town murmurs of kidnapping. Abduction. She swallowed, shook her head to clear it, but the thoughts kept on their familiar downward spiral.

She wasn't stupid. After three days with no leads on the case, statistics would predict that Tate was long gone. Ended up discarded in some ditch off Interstate 95, maybe in New Hampshire or Massachusetts if the guy got far enough with her. He'd had plenty of time, anyway. Three *days!* Tate's body would've had time to start decomposing with the help of the rain. Leo almost gagged. Eyes glazed and dull like a snake about to shed its skin but wide with the leftover terror of her own murder. Limbs all tangled and beautiful dark curls draped over an ashen face that was previously so warm and lips turned purple and bloody and *not Tate*. She'd know if they found a body, right? They'd tell her? Maybe that was what this impromptu cop intervention was about. *No. Fuck that. No no no.*

"She's not dead," Leo breathed.

"What's that?" The car sped up.

"Tate," Leo's voice cracked. "She's not. She can't be dead."

"Listen, kid—"

A blurred figure dashed out in front of the cruiser. The cop cursed and swerved, tires screeching, air roaring as the car broke free from the road. Seatbelt digging into her sternum. One deafening thunderclap against a telephone pole and they came to a violent stop.

Leo was frozen. She clutched her seat in a death grip that made her fingers ache later. Though unharmed, she realized from the sharpness in her throat that she'd been screaming. The figure they had avoided was printed on the backs of her eyelids.

The cop coughed, cursed again. "Y'alright?" he grumbled, staggering out of the car to open the backseat door and lean inside. His glasses had fallen off somewhere, revealing eyes so deeply set he gave the appearance of a bearded skeleton. Startling, if not for what had just happened.

Leo couldn't respond. She stared at him and felt tears run down her face.

"It was just a deer. Baby one." *Pronounced the "r" this time.* "The bastard scared me shitless." He straightened, groaning as he stretched his back and considered the damage to the car. The hood and front bumper were crumpled like discarded paper. "Sounded worse than it is, I think. Airbag didn't even go off. But I'll get someone else to drive you the rest of the way while I deal with this. I'm sorry you were here for it." He stepped away to make some calls. Passersby were rubbernecking the crash, slowing down to get a good look, and then resuming their journeys.

It wasn't a deer. Leo was more than positive. She released her fists from the fake leather seat and mechanically unbuckled her seatbelt. She'd seen her fair share of oblivious deer wandering into roads or in backyards. This was no fawn. Stepping out of the car with a grunt, she turned to the cemetery they had just passed. The mourning girl was gone. But there's no way she could have gotten from the middle of the cemetery to the road that fast. Leo glanced around. No deer. No woods close enough for it to have escaped into. The cemetery was several yards away now, the woods at its end impossibly distant.

A split second was all it took. Did that shadow really run out in front of the car, or was it there all along? Leo collapsed against the car door and nearly choked on a sob. She had seen Tate Mulder.

Except this was not a Tate she recognized. She was wearing the clothes which Leo had last seen her in; ripped blue jeans and a white long-sleeved Henley, one of her favorite outfits. The shirt used to be white, at least. When she had appeared in front of the car Leo had just enough time to see the tears in the fabric, the dirt and blood seeping through, the awful scrapes on her knees and worn-out sneakers. Far more akin to the Tate which had plagued Leo's nightmares as of late. But alive. She might have been crying. Her arms had hung at her sides, culminating in fists, as if approaching some menace head-on. Tate had always been one to confront her troubles without regard for consequences. It had to a greater extent led to more hurt than good, but Leo still admired her for it. Though in that moment the only challenger Tate seemed to be facing had been the police car which contained Leo and was hurtling headlong in her direction.

"Leonora?" The cop returned to the cruiser, where Leo was now feverishly wiping away her tears and trying to control her heart rate to steel herself for conversation. He'd found his sunglasses and restored his expressionless demeanor. "Another cruiser is almost here to pick you up," he said as if this fact was consoling, "And I called your aunt and uncle for you. They'll meet you at the station as soon as they can."

Leo had to stop herself from laughing through shuddering breaths. That ridiculous, hysterical, utterly inappropriate laugh that you may feel bubble up at funerals. She could imagine how that phone call went. Aunt Deborah would've picked up, most likely still wearing her obnoxious pink polka-dotted plush bathrobe, maybe her hair up in a towel. She worked earlier in the morning, so she was always there to see Leo get home after school. In her usual cheerful tone, she would answer, but then when the cop explained the situation over the phone, Leo visualized her aunt's voice raising an octave and demanding to speak to her niece with the utmost repugnance and venom in her words. The image conjured itself easily in Leo's mind: her aunt's eyes squeezed almost shut, nervous sweat beading along her brow, and a deep redness that extended down the woman's neck and into her bleach blonde hairline, her mouth flicking spit with every seething word as if she was going rabid. Here Leo supposed the anger was somewhat warranted, but this ferocious tone was used so often by her aunt for the smallest of issues that it had almost completely lost its power. That, and the fact that as Leo got older, she recognized that Deborah's physical demonstrations of fury more often than not far drowned out any sense that may have been present in her verbal attacks. It had been wielded as a weapon against anyone from salespeople to waiters who could not, for whatever reason, give Aunt Deborah what she wanted, which had often led to Leo breaking out into loud crying fits as a kid, which then in turn resulted in the rampage changing its target to her instead. Over the years she'd learned to accept the verbal blows with a blank face. As long as she waited it out, this seemed to work decently enough. At this point she was so detached she could mock the absurd episodes, though she wouldn't dare rise to her aunt's red-faced rage in person. But it was comically over the top, and she knew that now. The irate voice of Aunt Deborah was powerless against Leo; on the other hand, the cop looked a bit pale after this phone call, now that she thought about it. Sure enough, Leo felt the repetitive buzzing against her thigh which signified a barrage of panicked texts and missed calls.

Leo guessed that now wasn't a great time to explain to her aunt via text messages that some apparition of her missing girlfriend had caused a cop to crash his car with her inside. Or that the cop hadn't seen Tate at all. She ignored most of the texts for the moment and numbly typed a quick *I'm fine, see you at the station,* as the first big drops of rain splattered onto her phone screen.

The second cop who arrived to drive Leo the rest of the

way to her unwelcome destination was gracious enough to let the silence drag. She was relieved to be away from the veiled skeleton face of the first officer, but the relief was a minuscule feeling in comparison to the horrifying image of Tate, which would not leave her mind's eye.

Maybe it *had* been a deer, like the cop said. Maybe all Leo saw was a dark blur, and her distracted thoughts had filled in the blanks. She pressed the palms of her hands against closed eyes, leaned forward to pull against the seatbelt a little, wanting to rest her head between her legs. Make the nausea stop. There were far too many details to have mistaken the sight. As if the battered and victimized Tate was a photograph with the sharpness dialed all the way up. Too vivid but inconceivably real. The girl had stood out from the dull approaching storm at the point where it blended in with the monotone pavement. Still, enough light somehow to drape across her face and catch the wetness of the blood. Her familiarity was painful. The gentle hands which Leo had so ached to hold were scraped at the knuckles and curled in defiance. Her comforting brownish-gold gaze was hardened to deadly amber. The apparition was terrible and blunt. Like a kind of humanoid wraith. She was made undead without first passing entirely through death. One foot in the doorway to whatever comes next, and the other holding strong to this place. And now she was here to torment her lover. Leo recalled that her outline had been hazy. *Stop. Wraiths aren't real. Ghosts aren't real. Tate probably just ran away. Maybe someday she'll come back. I'm just—I'm scared* . . . Leo thought she had never been so scared in her life. The grotesque vision replayed on an endless loop.

She whipped upright in the backseat of the cruiser as if struck by lightning, hands whose tremors had now spread throughout Leo's body reaching her head as she stifled a groan.

It was Tate, but it couldn't have been. She had no shadow.

"DO YOU THINK we should put up a fence?" Leo asked over her shoulder as she scrubbed away at a plate in the sudsy kitchen sink.

Aunt Deborah filed her long nails without looking up. They were painted a gaudy neon pink, and the sound of the file on artificial nails coming from behind Leo's back made her wince. "For the millionth time, Leonora, Sebago is okay. She's a little wimp. Probably met a stray cat the other day and freaked out. We don't need a fence."

Leo set down the plate with a clang into the muddled water. "But the woods—"

"There's nothing in the woods." Her aunt's stare weighed heavily on Leo's shoulders. Sebbie trotted into the kitchen at the sound of her name and looked from Deb to Leo. The woman sighed at the dog. "Right, Sebago? You're just a wimp, huh?" Sebbie stretched out her forelegs and yawned, nudging her snout against Leo's ankle.

"She's not a wimp. But I'm not letting her go outside by herself for a while. Whatever it was could come back and hurt her worse." Unbidden, the image of Tate Mulder flashed behind her eyelids. Tate knelt next to Sebbie amongst the brush as the dog panted on her side, amber eyes widened to show the humanlike whites. The scratches on Sebbie's legs. And Tate's immovable gaze, fixed as if trying to make out details of the scene from a distance away with a hand draped over the dog's flank. Posed like a lethargic Renaissance painting made blurry by Leo's panic, with Tate staring off the canvas and then with the same intensity at Sebbie. One of those portraits that appear to see something formidable just behind you. That gaze made her uneasy. Tate must have seen whatever hurt Sebago, but it had been complete radio silence since the incident a few days ago.

"Will you stop being so paranoid? Christ." Deb stood from the kitchen table, her wooden chair protesting with the movement. Leo turned around and leaned against the laminate counter to face her, drying a knife with a rag. Sebago pricked up her ears and watched. "It's not healthy, honey. To be honest, it's annoying. Gonna give yourself a heart attack." She wobbled over to the living room, and Leo heard a soft thud as she hit the sofa.

Indeed. Leo lingered for a moment in the kitchen, catching her own eye in the reflection of the knife. Pale and far away. She dropped the knife in the cutlery drawer and bent down to pet Sebago behind the ears. A smile, a real one. "How about a walk, Sebbie?" The dog wagged her tail and pranced around Leo as she made her way over to where the leashes were kept. She trusted Sebago enough to stay close but wanted Aunt Deb to see her precaution. Seemed like Leo was the only one who cared about anything lately. If such a thing were possible. "We're gonna go see a friend," she said in a soft, excitable voice that she reserved only for her dog. Sebago woofed heartily and Leo agreed in earnest as she connected the leash to the leather collar and took off for the front door. Deb glared at her niece but said nothing along with her silent husband, in spite of the door slamming shut harder than Leo meant it to.

A friend. It truly touched Leo to see Tate caring about Sebago so much that day. But she wondered, and not for the first time: *why*.

While Leo led the way, it was as though Sebago already knew their destination, making all the necessary stops and turns unprompted. They had only been here once or twice before, for trick-or-treating when Leo was a kid and catching the bus to middle school before Aunt Deb had allowed her to walk by herself. The school bus would stop closer to Tate's house, at the intersection near the main road, and didn't bother going all the way down where the pavement turned to dirt and eventually led to Leo's place.

Now, as they approached Tate's driveway, Leo let go of the tattered leash and allowed Sebago to go on ahead toward the patio while she texted to let Tate know she was here. Thankfully it would be several hours before the early-summer brightness faded away. Then again, Sebago had been attacked in broad daylight.

Tate appeared in the doorway almost immediately, and Leo tried to hold back a small smile. "Huh, what have we here? Leo Bates making a house call? Didn't know that was possible," Tate said, leaning on the doorframe. Sebago circled Tate's bare feet, tail making her whole body wiggle with glee. She bent down to scratch between her ears. "How are you two?" Tate met Leo's eyes then, and her playfulness evaporated. She motioned for them to go to the other side of Tate's yard, where two makeshift swings hung from thick tree branches. The forest loomed behind the swings, sparse at first and then thicker.

"Was gonna ask you the same thing," Leo said. Each of the girls took a swing, which turned out to be simply two sanded-down planks of wood tied with rope. The wood and rope were softened over years of use and were surprisingly comfortable. The seats were the perfect size. Most swing sets, once you get older, feel like they were made for ants, impossibly low to the ground; these homemade swings, though, were situated high enough for both girls' feet to hang above the two dirt spots on the ground where the grass had been worn away by swinging sneakers. Sebago found a stick to gnaw and lay below their dangling feet, and Leo tried to think of how to start this conversation as silence stretched before them like a chasm.

She watched Sebago chew the stick below and was

E. M. ROY

stricken with heartache as her eyes rested on the faint healing scars on the dog's forelegs. A breath escaped her lips. "Tate, did you see whatever it was that hurt Sebbie?"

Tate glanced at Leo, hesitating. " . . . No," she said. The chasm opened up beneath them again, miles of silence threatening to swallow them whole. Leo felt very small, unable to touch the ground. Finally, Tate spoke again, but it caught Leo off guard. "You know I watched you after your parents died?"

The redhead flinched and met Tate's eyes sharply, the first eye contact they'd made since sitting on the swings. "What?"

"I think it was like a week or two after I heard about it. What were we, like, ten? But it was when you first came back to school after it happened. We were in different classes, but I watched you for a while. At recess and stuff. You were always alone. I wanted to say something but didn't really know what to say."

A gust of wind made the leaves and branches above them wave and rustle, and each swung in lazy accidental to-and-fros. Leo gripped the rope. "We didn't really know each other," she said quietly.

"Well, yeah. I *wanted* to know you, though," Tate said. "I saw you sitting in the field outside the school. The other kids kept their distance—I guess they just didn't know what to do with you after something like that, and kids are jerks, y'know. I was gonna go up and say hi, but I was nervous. Think I got a few feet behind you and realized you were picking dandelions." A small smile crept onto Tate's face. She wouldn't look at Leo. "You had a bunch laying out in a row and just kept counting them. I was sad for you."

Picking dandelions was an activity Leo often did in those weeks after losing her parents. She pictured a young Tate sneaking up behind her as she counted out the weeds, treating them with delicacy as if they were precious flowers.

"Then you ripped the heads off two of them and threw the stems away."

Leo had to laugh. "It messed me up for a while. As I'm sure you're aware. But then I got Sebbie-girl. She helped a lot." Sebago lifted her head, the now-gnarled stick between her jaws. Her dark tail wagged, and Leo patted her head. "Love an edgy backstory, right?"

Tate uttered a breathy chuckle that didn't do much to lighten the mood. "We do, we do," she agreed. "But I decided I better leave you alone. Everyone copes in weird ways. Weird shit."

"Yeah . . . it was definitely weird, what happened with them," Leo said. "And, uh. Terrifying." Her throat tightened and she shoved the thoughts from her mind. The circumstances of their deaths made her sick to think about.

Tate noticed Leo's change in demeanor and changed the focus to herself instead. "Something weird happened to me, too, back then. Around the same time, a little before I saw you with the dandelions. Obviously doesn't compare to your folks, but it was scary."

"What was it?" The keenness in Leo's voice surprised her. If Tate had something remotely traumatic happen to her in the past, Leo wanted to know. It could be a thread of similarity that would tie them closer together, sure, but it could also be one of the many keys to unlock one of the many locks that seemed to bar Tate from Leo's understanding. She wanted to know her. As selfish as that may be.

"I wandered off. In the woods. I was just playing, y'know, didn't feel like I'd gone far past the property line. I liked to play pretend; sometimes, I was Indiana Jones, or Lara Croft, or just an explorer charting new lands. Except the new lands were just in my backyard." She smiled then. "It was fun. It's nice to wander for a while. But when I turned around, I couldn't see my house anymore. I didn't think I'd gone that far, didn't realize I'd left the backyard, but I tried retracing my steps as best I could, and everything was just *trees*. So I started to panic and ran for what felt like miles. My family called the police when I didn't come home for dinner, and it took them a few hours to find me. By then, it was dark. And it was the kind of darkness where you can't tell the difference between the sky and the forest ahead of you. And I saw something there that really scared me. They only found me because they heard me screaming." Tate's gaze grew vacant.

Leo's heart thudded. "Well? What did you see?"

She was silent for a few beats too long. Then she wiped all traces of fear from her face in an instant and replaced them with a smirk and a shrug. Leo could almost hear the click of a key turning in a lock. "I don't remember. The cops who found me said later that there was a dead deer nearby, and I probably ran into that. All mangled and decomposing. I guess that explains how I found blood on my shoes later. And then—" Tate squinted in thought and looked up at the looming branches. "I remember throwing the shoes as far into the woods as I could without walking in again myself. No idea why. It felt like they weren't mine anymore."

Her shoulders relaxed, releasing the breath she'd been holding. Leo stood, hands in her pockets and stumbling a bit as she stepped from the height of the swing. Sebago looked up at her curiously. "Yep, that's pretty weird." She laughed as Tate let out an exclamation of indignation. The story had amused her—at least, it was easier to act amused. Childhood superstition mixed with an overactive imagination, that's all. Leo decided to play along. "Maybe whatever hurt Sebbie is whatever you saw when you were a kid, eh? Like a demon." She kicked at Tate's dangling bare feet playfully.

Tate giggled but tensed her frame. "Nah. I think me and the woods of good old Eston just aren't on the best of terms."

Leo thought about her parents again. That happened in the woods, too. "I get that," she said. "They probably don't like me much either, then."

"Y'know," Tate began. She looked down, not meeting

Leo's eyes. "I've been doing some research lately. On Eston, and the woods." Her fingers played with the fraying rope of the swing. Then she looked up at Leo through her eyelashes and smirked. "Maybe I'll show you sometime. Call it a date."

This prompted a blink and a blush from Leo, but Tate continued before she could question it. "Just sucks that poor Sebbie had to be the one the woods chose to pick on this time. She did nothing wrong." Tate jumped down from her swing and rubbed Sebago's scruff vigorously with both hands. Leo smiled at the dog's obvious joy at the attention. Then Tate met her eyes again, shivering with the start of the evening chill. "Why us, anyway?"

Leo took off her sweatshirt and draped it around Tate's shoulders without comment. "I dunno. Guess we're special." The way that the girl spoke of the woods around town was unnerving, but Tate's previous words smoothed down her prickling apprehension like a grindstone: *Call it a date.* She watched as her slender fingers felt the soft lining of Leo's sweatshirt.

After a moment, Tate rose to her feet and moved in close. She grinned and pulled Leo in for a hug. In her surprise, Leo wrapped her arms around her waist and held on tight to the girl. Her own phantom heat still permeated the sweatshirt that now covered Tate, re-warming Leo's hands in the embrace. Her quiet words over Leo's shoulder disturbed some of the flyaway strands of fiery hair that had escaped Leo's knot. "I guess we are."

THIS SECOND ATTEMPT at a ride to the police station was rather uneventful. All the same, Leo could not shake the feeling of being watched. Almost every time she glanced up, the cop's stare in the rearview mirror quickly flitted back to the road, and more than one pedestrian looked on at the cruiser for a little too long as it passed from the sidewalk. An old man leaned against the doorframe of a small shop in the town's center, smoking and watching the traffic go by along the disorganized double intersection. A couple of kids walking back from school locked eyes with Leo through the window of the cruiser as it passed. She could've sworn the windows were blacked out on the outside.

It was finally raining by the time they arrived at the station. Leo found herself pinching the delicate skin of her inner forearm. Red marks bloomed under the skin in the shape of her fingertips and bitten-down nails. She didn't feel it. She decided to break the silence. "Did they find something bad?" Her glare pierced through the grate separating the back seat from the front, searching for the slightest reaction in the rearview from the second cop she'd had the displeasure of interacting with today. *Because I think I just did.* Except she was exhausted, so she'd only imagined a wraithlike Tate in the road, of course. Obviously. There was no shadow on the pavement where she stood, despite the final rays of light before the rainstorm reflecting off still-fresh blood dripping from her curly hairline and across her crooked nose. Not dead and not alive. No shadow.

"Not my job to tell you that, miss," he grumbled, annoyed. He pulled into a space and shifted the car into park with a slight squeak of the brakes, rain splattering in weighty drops on the roof and windshield. The trees which surrounded the far side of the police station and parking lot swayed against the melancholic sky overhead, water dripping from their branches in thicker bursts.

A flash of impatience brought color to Leo's cheeks, and she pinched her forearm harder, hugging her arms around herself. "Pretty sure that's your only job right now, actually," she said through gritted teeth.

The officer turned around in the driver's seat to face her with an arm against the back of the passenger's seat, his expression fragmented by the grate between them. This cop was clean-shaven, with acne scars patrolling his jawline. He probably wasn't more than ten years older than Leo. She made a note not to ask what the guy's last name was; she didn't need another probable relative of a classmate to loathe. "You think every cop gets briefed on every single investigation going on? That doesn't happen. We follow our orders. I know as much as you do at this point, kid," he said. Doubt that. "They're looking for Tate Mulder. And they want some information they seem to think you have. I was told to come get you after that geriatric idiot bumped his cruiser on a telephone pole. And now the department's gonna have to pay for that shit. That's all I know. Don't gotta be so suspicious." He got out and slammed the car door before opening one in the back and gesturing for her to step out. The previous officer with the obscured face didn't seem to be terribly old, but Leo was just impressed that this one knew the word "geriatric," especially if he had indeed attended her high school.

Leo tied her oversized flannel around her waist before stepping out of the car and loosely shrugged on her jacket. She was cold with sweat at this point, and the rain wasn't helping. At the same time, the cop shut the back door of the car, the police station's front doors swung open, and a woman stepped outside. She had a hand to her face, wiping away tears in a way that obscured any other distinguishing features from view. Unbothered by the impending downpour, her black hair hung about her shoulders in tight braids that were beginning to fray. A stout man with thin glasses walked halfway through the double doors after her but apparently thought better of pursuing any further and simply watched her retreat into the parking lot. He shot a glance in Leo's direction and promptly disappeared inside the building.

The woman neared Leo and the cop and slowed her pace. "Leo?" Her hand curled around the hem of her thick jacket, immaculately-painted nails hiding themselves inside.

The cop beside her grunted with frustration. Leo ignored him, stunned at the sound of the woman's familiar voice as she drew closer. Recognition clicked. "Miss Mulder—"

"Oh, you know you can call me Marion, sweetie." Tate's mother enveloped her in a firm hug, bending down a bit so that she wasn't towering over Leo too much. Her heart ached. They both felt the missing space between them as sore as a bruise, even as they held each other close. Like if they held on tight enough, they could find Tate within one another.

"Ma'am, I need to get Miss Bates inside." The cop tried to usher Leo toward the station.

Marion Mulder whipped around and snapped at him with such ferocity that Leo tensed and felt much smaller than usual standing by her side. Lips almost drawn back in a snarl, she said, "Fuck off. I'll tell you when we're ready."

This seemed to have caught the impatient officer off guard. He took a few startled steps away and crossed his arms, waiting. "Two minutes."

The woman sighed and turned her attention back to Leo, leaning down to plant a maternal kiss on the crown of her head. It was the first time Leo felt any semblance of comfort that day. That week, that month. Her eyes stung as she welcomed it warmly.

"Cops suck, huh?" Marion joked in a sad whisper. Then she sniffled, smoothing out the arms of Leo's coat. "They were, ah—pretty harsh in there."

"Why were they harsh to you? Tate's your daughter," Leo said, defensive on the woman's behalf.

"Just trying everything, I guess. I don't blame them. At least they're doing their job—though I already told them everything. She just wasn't in her room that morning, and that was it. Today they brought in some detective from Boston, and he wanted to do more interviews with the same people. I think it's . . . it might be getting more serious. Oh, god," Marion wiped at her face before any tears could trickle down. Her face was a mirror of Tate's, round with intense features, and eyes that could look directly into your soul. Though her nose was perfectly straight and contoured. Tate's was set at a slight angle that made her all the more endearing. Leo found herself touching the smooth bridge of her own nose while she considered this and hated herself distantly. Marion continued. "I just want Tate to be okay. My Tater-tot—she doesn't even *have* to come home if she really doesn't want to, if she did run away—I trust her, she's a strong girl who can make it on her own, you know that. I just want to *know* that she's okay." She chuckled despite the glassiness of her eyes.

Leo didn't want to add to the woman's pain, so she held back her own tears. *Tater-tot*. The sweet nickname would've made Leo snicker under different circumstances. Undoubtedly one she'd used to address a littler Tate, a softer Tate, a Tate whose main concerns in life were skinned knees and popsicles. Leo had never known this Tate.

She didn't know what she could ever say to comfort Marion. Why would Tate leave them both? The two people who cared so much? She wanted to leave the safe familiarity of Eston; she'd said so before, but would she actually do it? It was something that Leo went back and forth on every hour as her grief chased frustration around her head like a cat and mouse. She didn't dare vocalize the question to Tate's mom.

At the hesitation, Marion spoke again, in a lower voice as she stooped down to whisper a small distance from Leo's ear. "I don't want you to blame yourself, Leo. Never do it." Leo was taken aback. "I know you and Tate have a very special relationship—hell, the way she talks about you, that's a love I've never experienced, and I'm so glad she has you. She was just so secretive sometimes—" She turned away to take a shuddering breath. A warmth cascaded down Leo's cheeks, and the world went blurry. "I *know* you, sweetie. I care about you a lot; you've dealt with your share of pain over the years. But, just . . . if you know anything about my Tate, please tell someone," she said.

Leo took a step backward and stared at Marion with her heart pounding. The half-forgotten cop then grumbled that it was time to go into the station. She hastily wiped her face. *I don't know. I don't know anything. Do you?* She couldn't form a sentence. Marion pulled her in for a final embrace and then briskly trotted to her car without waiting for a response.

BEFORE

EO'S CALLUSED FINGERS touched each string without hesitation. This was a beat she was well acquainted with. The notes presented themselves of their own volition, humming out smoothly and deeply. The corners of her lips twitched as she felt the vibrations pass from her bass guitar and dance over her skin, warming her fingertips in an electric embrace.

Without stopping the song or missing a beat, Leo turned her attention from the strings to the girl sitting on the floor by her legs. Tate was mesmerized, and Leo felt a lovely sort of satisfaction. This was all she needed. Thrumming a steady, familiar beat on her old red bass (which had actually been her mother's—her late parents were both locally-successful musicians in their prime, rarities in Eston) to an audience of one. Or, she supposed two—Sebago lay curled in the corner of Leo's bed, fast asleep, trail draped over her snout. The song Leo was playing wasn't that complicated; an *OK Computer*-era Radiohead tune that Leo had been particularly fond of in middle school and still loved today. But playing for Tate somehow heightened Leo's skill. She was hyperaware of just about everything in her small bedroom, it seemed, except for the subtle beat her fingers produced. The rise and fall of Sebbie's chest, the absentminded way that Tate picked at her cuticles as she listened. The strumming was a matter of pure muscle memory and, where she missed a note or two, the unthinking and natural improvisation which can only accompany the unnaturally talented. Tate was usually not familiar enough with the songs Leo played to pick up on these substitutions, but she did see a confident deftness in Leo's playing, which was not expressed in any other setting of her life. If Leo pursued music professionally when they were real adults, she might even have a shot, and Tate recognized this. The music was a living thing, and she was the lightning that struck its corpse. After a long break of wordless thrumming from Leo's bass, Tate was finally moved to speak.

"You need to write your own music." Her gaze moved slowly from Leo's resting hands to meet her eyes.

Leo huffed and rubbed the back of her neck. "Not sure I work that way. I can parrot back basslines from songs I like, but I've never made up my own." This was only half-true. Leo knew she was sometimes capable of improvising certain notes at a time, but her original music endeavors had never gone beyond the point of filling in the gaps in her memory.

"Well, you should try. It'd be *amazing*, dude." Tate leaned against the side of Leo's bed where she sat, cradling her bass like a precious thing. Where her arm touched Leo's leg radiated a delicious warmth that Leo tried to ignore. Sebbie snored gently beside her.

Playing bass was a nostalgic kind of medication, she thought. It reminded her of her parents, sure, but more than that, her private sessions acted as a self-soothing practice, hypnotic at times. She could stop paying attention to the movement of her fingers and just let them play for hours. As if she was watching herself from afar, like a constant captive audience. It was nice sometimes to be outside her body. When Tate noticed the pretty red instrument looming in the corner of Leo's small bedroom and started asking to hear her play whenever she visited (still a strange and new occurrence), the listener seemed occasionally entranced as well. Leo loved it. One may not always hear the bass upfront in many songs, but without it, the song was nothing. A subtle background beat giving structure to the whole. The timekeeper.

Leo looked out of the singular window of her grayish room. July sunlight struck the glass through the lush trees not far from her aunt's house. She furrowed her brow slightly in thought. "I don't even know what I would write songs about."

Tate considered this. "Whatever strikes you as important, I guess. School. Graduating. I dunno. *Love*." She grinned mischievously at this last syllable and Leo's face grew hot, redness spreading from her cheeks all the way to her similarly colored hairline. "But what do I know? I don't really have anything like that. Honestly, if you wrote a song about the sandwich you had for lunch, I'd think it was the most profound shit I ever heard."

Leo chuckled and found that her fingers had begun plucking at the strings again nervously. No particular song, just a quiet walking beat. She didn't mind Tate's teasing—in fact, she often savored it, which she would never admit to anyone—but she did wonder if Tate actually picked up on Leo's attraction or if these were just convenient jokes. The memory of Tate's coming out being interrupted by Leo getting a speeding ticket about a month ago resurfaced, and Leo smirked. They were the too-sweet taste of a love before it's ripe.

A loud *thump* came from outside Leo's window. Both girls flinched, Leo especially as she had started falling into her familiar bass-playing daze and was jerked out of it so abruptly. Sebago jerked awake, ears pricked and alert. "The hell was that?" Tate stood to walk toward the glass. Then another thump. And another.

Sebago barked and jumped down from Leo's bed, landing just beneath the windowsill. Black blurs crossed the small field of vision that the solitary window provided. Too quick to identify and too many to count. The girls looked at each other in frightened confusion. The room vibrated, the glass clattering. A sharp, spiderwebbed crack stretched over the surface. Red smears with each hit.

Several more thumps in quick succession, growing louder and more violent, a sound filling the room with something like high-pitched screams, Sebago barking, the din reaching a crescendo, deafening, and then silence.

Leo didn't dare move any closer but kept her gaze fixed, waiting for another barrage of blows. It never came. "Is someone outside?" she asked when it seemed to be over. The dog growled.

Tate looked out the window from the side so she wasn't facing it head-on. There was only one floor to Leo's house; the thought of someone breaking the glass was feasible and made her palms sweat. She watched as Tate's jaw dropped, and she moved to get a better look at something on the ground, forehead pressing against the pane. "Oh my god, they're birds," she said.

Leo and Tate ran out and around the house, and sure enough, the bodies of seven crows lay unresponsive beneath Leo's bedroom window. Most of the crows had their necks bent at grotesque angles.

After a silence, Leo swallowed and spoke with false lightness, "I thought crows were supposed to be smart. These guys just, like . . . "

"And only your room," Tate said. Her eyes were threatening to overflow with tears, but her voice was steady. None of the other windows on this side of the house had crows laying beneath it. Specks of blood and black feathers littered the off-white siding of the house, all aiming toward Leo's window and spattered across it. Sebago was standing up on her hind legs from inside Leo's room, paws leaning on the windowsill, so she could watch over the two girls. They could hear her anxious whines through the glass. Blood and feathers obscured the dog's view like an abhorrent mosaic.

All they could do was stare at the birds. Leo hoped that Tate wouldn't cry. The girl hugged her arms around herself tightly. Then Tate took a breath and uttered one slightly amused word. "Murder."

Leo flinched. "What?"

"A group of crows."

Tate knelt closer to the birds' corpses. She wiped the tears from her eyes with the hem of her shirt. "Hey, it's okay, let's go inside—" Leo said, placing a hand on Tate's shoulder. Ignoring her, Tate gently stroked the feathers of one of the crows' folded, crumpled wings. She extended the limb slowly. Leo was startled. "Don't touch that, dude! What the fuck?" She tightened her grip on the crouching girl's shoulder.

"It's like the beginning of a horror movie," Tate said. She held the extended wing so delicately. Feathers splayed. Like Adam reaching out to God's hand, all ballet fingers and elegance in desperation. Sympathy made her voice shaky and quiet, but there was also something else there. Wonder. "You know? In the first act. A bunch of birds fly over the house and die, or all the fish in a lake. It's, a sign of the apocalypse, or the devil, or a curse. *Pestilence*." She breathed the last word as if it stung. "You don't happen to live on an ancient Native American burial ground, do you?" Tate finally turned to Leo and smirked.

"I don't, and that's a cheap trope." Leo watched as Tate ever-so-softly returned the wing to its original folded position by the dead bird's side. "Wouldn't have pegged you as such a weirdo, honestly."

She laughed. "Damn, that's cold, Bates. Pretty sure you're the weirdo here." Tate stood up, close enough for Leo to feel her warmth. "I feel bad just leaving them like this. What do we do?"

"I'll tell my uncle when he gets home." Leo resisted the urge to tug on Tate's sleeve and scowled instead, arms tensed. "Let's go inside."

Tate didn't stay at Leo's place much longer after that. She was distracted, gaze distant, and finally excused herself on the pretense of running an unspecified errand. Undefined guilt gnawed at Leo's stomach as she watched Tate walk down the driveway. She'd taken something out of her bag while she was walking, a notebook of some kind, and looked like she was writing something down before she turned the corner of the dirt road and was out of sight.

Later, Leo could see the faint shadow of Uncle Mike at the edge of the woods, shovel in hand, and the last of the crow corpses slumped in the spade. He melted with it into the long-limbed trees and became indistinguishable from the night.

AFTER

THE POLICE STATION smelled of sickness and tension. The air was thick with underlying despondence not dissimilar to that of a hospital, but at least in a hospital, there's some sense of resilience—whereas here, this was replaced by disheartening smudges on the linoleum floors and unidentified murmurs coming from behind the two-way mirror. This was a place where one cannot step out of line at the risk of one's credibility and promised safety. Leo could not meet her own eyes in the two-way mirror for fear of what lay beyond.

She hated herself for flinching as the door to the small room opened and willed a sort of calmness over her body. No need to be so goddamn jumpy. While the place was rather dreary and the few faces she'd seen on the way in hadn't seemed the warmest, she was only here to help give some information about Tate. That's all.

A stout man entered the room where Leo had been waiting for about twenty minutes (which was the perfect allotment of time to give the pit in her stomach a chance to grow into an absolute black hole of anxiety, thank you very much). It was the same man who had followed Marion to the exit and watched her leave the station. The man who made Tate's mother cry. "Hello there, Leonora," he said, shuffling a file as he shut the door behind him with a flat slam.

"Just Leo's okay."

"Okay then, 'Just Leo,'" he smirked. Leo disliked him

already. Her eyes followed the small stack of papers as he placed them on the table, out of reach for the moment. "I'm Detective Ander. I was called up here from Boston to help with investigating the disappearance of Tate Mulder."

Detective Ander seemed to be waiting for a reaction from over his thin-framed spectacles. Leo met his gaze. "Yeah, you didn't seem like you're from around here."

Luckily, he chuckled. "The outfit not working for you?" Corporate and impeccable. It wasn't.

"Nah, you just speak more clearly. You enunciate." Leo folded her hands on the chilled table.

"I'll take that as a compliment." The detective finally took a seat across from Leo, which she took as a sign that she'd passed the entrance exam. He coughed, and Leo smelled the distinct tang of cigarettes. "I take it you are very close with Miss Mulder?"

Leo blinked with slight incredulity. "She's my girlfriend," she said. "I said that to the other guys earlier. When it first happened a few days ago."

"Yes, that's what I was told." Detective Ander patted the neatly-packed file in front of him. "I'm just going to jump right into it, if you don't mind. You seem like a smart girl, so I won't waste your time. Tell me honestly now, did Tate ever speak to you about running away? Did she have a plan?"

So she could still be alive. Leo felt her posture change as some of the fear released its grip on her lungs. Their newfound evidence wasn't a body; Tate could be okay. "Well, we all do," she said. "I've talked about this before. Nobody *wants* to stay in Eston. After school, she was thinking about college in New York. Or Boston. Running away would've meant going there sooner, I guess."

"I see." Detective Ander's voice remained polite. She was telling him things he already knew. His bespectacled gaze drifted back to the papers as Leo tried to read his expression. He then leaned forward with a decided exhale, folding his hands over the papers in what Leo realized was a mirror of her own current stance. The gray in the man's trimmed hair was more prominent than she first thought. "Leo, you and I both know there's more to this."

Leo's eyes widened. "I—"

"I know that you and Miss Mulder were having problems at school. Can you tell me about that?"

"Oh," she said. Problems at school? "Uh. Tate wasn't— isn't. Everyone likes her. I keep my distance, I guess. We only got to know each other over the summer."

"Right. Tate *wasn't* having school troubles, for certain. Good grades and plenty of friends." The man adjusted his glasses and flipped a page. "So, then, what was the high school outcast—" he gestured to Leo, "—doing with the popular girl all summer?"

She tensed her shoulders. "I'm not sure."

"Were you bullied at school, Leo? For being a lesbian?" His gaze was unrelenting.

"What?" she said. "No, I wasn't." She certainly wouldn't tell this old, straight Bostonian man if she was facing any type of discrimination in Eston. Other things, darker things, had taken precedence over Leo's sexuality in terms of the perception her peers had of her. The earlier hallucination of Tate standing in the road, bloody and defiant, flashed through her mind, raising goosebumps on her arms. It *was* a hallucination. Stress-induced. She was thankful it didn't happen at school where others could spectate. "And Tate wasn't bullied for that, either. She wasn't even out in that environment yet. She got some racism, though. The implicit kind."

"Despicable." Detective Ander folded his arms. Leo bit her tongue. "Certainly a reason to run away. But, you see, there's one thing I can't wrap my head around. Say Tate did run away. She's off camping out in some cheap New York motel. I can get that. We have some folks keeping an eye on places like that right now. But . . . *you're* still here, Leo. Why is that?"

Leo blanched. It was a question that had been itching

in the back of her mind like a splinter these three days since Tate's disappearance. A splinter—perhaps more akin to shrapnel—cutting deeper every day and leaving poisonous thoughts in its wake. A dull anger bubbled up Leo's spine. If she ran away . . . *She didn't even* tell *me. She just left me here.* And her mother, too. For the first time, her frustration overtook the grief. She felt betrayed. Confused. "I don't know. I couldn't tell you why that is."

The detective leaned forward again, dissecting Leo's reaction syllable by syllable. His cigarette breath made Leo want to hold her own. The memories that arose with that scent were too much to bear. Smoking in the woods with Tate. Sharing stolen cigarettes and kisses. She winced. Then the detective's voice softened. "I want you to know that I'm on your side. We both want the same thing, my friend. To find Tate safe and sound. There are things you aren't telling me, though. I'm not pulling any punches here, and I invite you to do the same." He smiled and opened his arms in a welcoming gesture.

"Not sure what you're implying." The smile didn't reach his eyes.

He cleared his throat and flipped over the thin file. A single sheet of paper was selected as he adjusted his spectacles. "'History of violence,'" he read. "Says here that you hurt another student this past summer."

Pushed to the ground. A face blocking out the sun. Vicious laughter and a kick to the stomach. So he did know about the homophobia, after all.

At Leo's silence, Detective Ander resumed. "Tragedies beget tragedies, don't they?" Startled, Leo heard the same words in the officer's voice, muffled by the beard and sunglasses which obscured a skeletal face just a few moments before Tate had made him crash the cruiser. No, a deer. Right? "Do you lose your temper often, Leo?"

"Do I lose my temper?" All rational thought abandoned Leo's mind, leaving her body to fester in its rapidly boiling panic. She could barely grasp the tendrils of the vile idea which began to take root. The detective couldn't mean what she thought he did. Tate's shadowless figure in the middle of the road. Looking at her. "You're—you think that I . . . "

He watched Leo without blinking and soaked in every square inch of her body language. Read her like a book. Hopefully one that had its most important pages ripped out. "I'm unsure if you *meant* to do anything, of course, or perhaps weren't *aware* of what you were doing. But I think that you and Tate had an argument the night she disappeared. I think you got angry with her. And then maybe she ran to protect herself. Or maybe you got to her first."

Something at the edge of Leo's memory. A glimmer that took the shape of tall, spindly trees, pulled and bent toward a magnetic center, crackling branches, a silhouette . . .

Before Leo could think of a response—she had no idea what she could've said to make her case better, anyway— the metal door to the holding room burst open, and Aunt Deborah barreled through, a red-faced Uncle Mike and a tired officer trailing behind her in the doorway. Detective Ander appeared unbothered, only shooting one stern glare at the officer, who muttered an apology. *"Leonora Bates!* You don't say another word without a lawyer, honey," Deb exclaimed, rushing over to where Leo sat and running a sweaty hand through her niece's hair, which had found its way out of its usual knot at some point.

"Can I assume you are Leo's guardians?" Detective Ander asked, placing the papers back within their manila folder.

Aunt Deb gripped Leo's shoulders. She would have recoiled from the touch if she hadn't been so shocked. "I think you've done enough *assuming,* sir! Just what do you think you're doing, interrogating an eighteen-year-old girl without a lawyer—look how pale she is! This is *cruelty!*" A hand tried to tilt Leo's chin up to look her aunt in the eye, but Leo remained frozen, staring at the detective and his file.

"She's not under arrest, ma'am," Detective Ander said. "I asked her a few questions and she answered willingly. Now, I need to run an errand, and then we will finish up. You're welcome to sit in here with her while I'm gone." He packed the file and rose from the space across the table from Leo.

"Is this legal?" Uncle Mike spoke up for the first time, the crackly voice resounding from his uncertain place behind the officer in the doorway.

"What, keeping her here at the station? Yes, the girl is an adult," Detective Ander said. "Of course, Leo isn't being held against her will. But, in all honesty, I don't think it would look great on her part if she left without us finishing our little chat." He winked at Leo then, and she barely had the energy to be disgusted.

BEFORE

"I'M GOING TO see Tate. Be back for dinner," Leo called on her way out the door.

"You've been spending a lot of time with that girl, huh?" Aunt Deborah replied from the kitchen. There was no negative tone in her voice, but Leo knew the woman well enough to picture the expression on her face. Sebago watched her approach from a pillow on the living room floor.

Leo stopped with one foot outside, headed toward her rusty car. She chose her words cautiously. "Yeah, I guess." In fact, the two girls had spent several days a week together since Tate showed up in Leo's driveway at the end of June. The realization brought with it a gentle thrill.

There was seldom any explicit conversation between Leo and her guardians regarding her sexuality, but she also had never tried to hide it. In the simplest way, she had figured and hoped that her primary school playground stints of kissing games with the other girls had given her family the message. Thankfully, it had. Aunt Deborah and Uncle Mike were pretty much indifferent these days. This was Eston, Maine, anyway, not the deep South. It's not as though she would be kicked out, or punished. Things like that did not happen here.

"I just don't want you to get hurt, honey. I don't want trouble for you." Deb had moved from the kitchen down a step to where Leo could see her in their small living room. Mike flipped through the TV from his cracked leather recliner with no comment.

"Tate is the opposite of trouble," Leo said, the end of her statement going up a little in an anxious half-question.

"I'm sure she's great, dear." *Dee-yah*. "But you be careful."

Leo furrowed her brow. "'Kay, Deb." Sebbie sat up then and licked Leo's hand. "I'm okay, baby," she whispered to the dog with a scratch behind the ear, hoping her aunt and uncle wouldn't hear the consolation. She swung open the outer metal door all the way and bounced down the wooden porch. Deb meant well, she supposed. When she kept her temper, at least. If Leo had protested her aunt's implications, there likely would have been an argument that ended in her not being allowed to leave the house, and she couldn't risk not seeing Tate.

In a split-second decision, Leo veered left away from her car and instead picked up her skateboard from its accustomed place leaning against the front of the house. There was only about a fifteen-minute walk between Leo's house and Tate's; could be nice to get some air. She was early as always, anyway. Her board was a beat-up old longboard with several chips in the front and back from innumerable attempts at tricks and inevitable falls. Fondly she remembered her parents giving her this board for her tenth birthday, at that time looking daunting and huge. Her mother had held her shaky hands and walked her up and down their paved driveway on the unsteady board until she'd felt comfortable enough to stand on her own and do nervous little pushes with her back foot. They laughed, but Leo had been determined after seeing some TV show where a boy did a bunch of tricks on a skateboard. That kind of childhood fixation on a random subject that suddenly occupies most of their waking thoughts until they've explored the thing to death and nigh-on mastered it. For Leo, this was skateboarding and, more intensely a handful of years later, bass guitar. Her tenth was the final birthday she had spent together with her parents, her skateboard the last gift they had given her.

The rumble of the worn wheels over uneven pavement was a suitable white noise to anchor Leo to the ground, to the world, to Eston, while her thoughts drifted to Tate as they so often did these past few weeks. Today was the day she would confess. Though she hadn't woken up that morning with the intention, she felt it now, riding to her best friend's house with the wind unraveling strands of her knotted-up hair like it was any other day. A dreamy grin touched her lips as she glided along the old paved road.

In retrospect, she supposed her feelings were rather obvious. Especially after that speeding ticket she'd gotten. But naivety granted her the current bliss of believing no one else noticed how her eyes followed Tate across the room, or the softness in her voice which was brought out by Tate and Tate alone.

"Hey there!"

Leo, all but floating away on the sweet possibility of reciprocated love, jumped and stopped her board. The voice sounded familiar, but she didn't place it at first.

A boy about her age drifted out on a bike from a driveway she had just passed, hopping up and circling ahead of Leo on the sidewalk. "What's up, babe? Where you going, lookin' so happy?" Recognition flashed across his eyes as he came to a stop. "Oh, you were in my English class! Leo, right?"

"Yeah." She bit her lip. "And you're Jonathan. Talbot."

"That's me!" The blond boy propped his bike on the kickstand. They were only a block or two away from Tate's house. Leo tried to think of an escape script. The boy had seemed normal enough in class. He was probably harmless, if a little forward. "Hey, do you know what the summer reading is?"

"Yeah. *Macbeth.*"

"Oh, right. Hate that book. Not that I've read it, or plan on it." He chuckled to himself. Leo looked behind him at Tate's house past the trees in the distance. "What, not even a smile?" He pointed to his grin cartoonishly. Then dropped the act, fidgeting with the hem of his shirt before looking down at Leo directly. "I think your parents used to be friends with my aunt and uncle, you know. We could've been pals."

Her brow furrowed. This wasn't how she'd thought a conversation with this kid would go. "I think you're thinking of someone else, man." Her parents weren't exactly around anymore to keep up with friends.

"No, I'm definitely not," Jonathan leaned back on his bike, which teetered dangerously. "My mom had an older brother and sister. They were twins. Bryce and Mackenzie."

Of course. Bryce and Mackenzie Talbot. Leo swallowed.

The boy must have seen the realization in Leo's eyes. "Yeah. Did your mom and pop ever tell you what happened to the Talbot twins before they bit the dust?"

She looked behind Jonathan and to the trees at the side of the road to her left, muscles tensed. "I heard they got into an accident," she said lamely.

He scoffed. "I guess you could call it that. If murder can be an accident, then yeah, sure."

Leo's heart dropped. She gripped her skateboard on the shelf of her hips. Murder? "I don't know what the fuck you're talking about."

"Then you're just as crazy as your batshit mom was." Her stomach churned, and she suddenly felt very ill. "Ava Bates and her little pet Kenneth White killed my aunt and uncle when they were eighteen."

"Is this a fucking joke?" Leo gritted her teeth to keep from screaming the words.

Jonathan approached her. His Vineyard Vines shirt was wrinkled at the collar, and he stank of body spray. "But you know what? I'm a forgiving type. You clearly owe me a debt, and I will gladly accept it, because I'm *so* charitable." He adjusted his hair and took another step closer. "I know we didn't talk a lot in class, but maybe you could come hang out. We can get to know each other? It's only fair. Do the summer reading together and, uh—other stuff." He looked her up and down.

She could barely follow the conversation. Leo forced a smile that didn't reach her eyes and felt grotesque and suffocating. "No. I'm busy. And I've already read *Macbeth*." She dropped her board and started to skate away.

"Yo, wait! Are the rumors true, then? The other ones, I mean. Not about your dead parents." He snickered.

She froze and turned around. "What rumors?"

A mischievous, arrogant grin took over his face. "Not only was your mom insane, and probably passed it down to you, but I also heard you were a dyke. If you and your girl want a man to join ya, spice things up a little, I'm down."

Leo stared at the boy, mouth agape. This was an interaction she'd only ever seen online or from the safe distance that fiction provided. People weren't supposed to be like this in real life.

At her stunned silence, Jonathan chuckled. His gait was confident, and he reached out a thin hand to brush Leo's hip. She backed away as if stabbed. "Oh, come on," Jonathan said. "People have seen you around town, you know. With Tate Mulder. Now *that's* crazy. That you somehow pulled the hot black chick before me or the other guys could wear her down. I bet she's fun; it's always the popular ones with great tits who end up being freaky. I'd love to help you both out, so you won't need a strap-on anymore—"

The shock which froze Leo initially was then converted to vicious rage. Warmth bubbled up her chest and spread across her face. Her hands shook, nails digging into palms without an ounce of feeling. It was as if she was watching it all from afar; she felt entirely outside of herself. Entirely *other*. Spectating her own life, no longer the one in control, no longer the one driving, on the edge of her seat waiting to see whatever shit she'd get herself into this time.

She punched him.

A satisfying *crack* rippled across Jonathan's cheekbone, and Leo could feel his teeth crunch against her knuckles from the inner side of his cheek. The boy looked surprised, did a half-spin with the momentum, and stumbled back. Blood trickled from a split lip, and a threatening redness approached his eye. Leo figured her knuckles were probably cut and bleeding too, but she felt nothing save an exhilarated vengeance.

Drifting, drifting away, and watching from afar. The separation between the physical Leo, standing there with an ache that spread diligently up her right arm, and conscious thought, felt altogether too easy and intoxicating. She was dimly aware that she should have been more frightened. Instead, the adrenaline and anger carried her into a high of blissful violence.

Three crows chattered amongst themselves a short distance away from the scuffle on the sidewalk, which seemed to be paused in time. Leo could almost smile at them in her delirium.

Jonathan stood up straight and wiped his mouth. The shirtsleeve came away red. He said something that Leo didn't catch through the white ringing in her ears.

He laughed and shoved her to the ground. Her back hit the edge of the idle skateboard, rolling it toward the trio of crows, who scattered into the air. A murder of otherworldly creatures. Leo watched them fly off as if she was stargazing.

When shall we three meet again?

A kick to the gut.

In thunder, lightning, or in rain?

Just stay still. Another kick, a crack, a wheeze. A shout in the distance.

Fair is foul and foul is fair—

"Hey, what the fuck?! Get *away* from her!" Tate pushed Jonathan aside with a force he wasn't expecting; he lurched into the grass beyond the sidewalk, then guffawed at her out-of-breath fury.

"Have fun with your bitch, dyke," he barked over his

shoulder, hopping back on his bike and pedaling away with a careless lack of haste.

Tate yelled something vulgar after the boy as she crouched to Leo's crumpled form on the pavement. The distance was closing back in now, the high wearing off; her knuckles pounded in time with her racing heart, and shockwaves of pain emanated from her ribcage. Gentle hands brushed the hair out of her face. "Leo, should I call 9-1-1? I don't know what to do. Are you okay to stand? Is anything broken?" Leo could hear the tears in Tate's voice.

Leo took a shaky breath and stopped cradling her stomach, rolling onto her back with a groan. She met Tate's dark and terrified eyes staring down from above, blocking out the sun. And Leo grinned. The sunlight caught Tate's curly flyaways in the most endearing way. Like the edges of her being were on fire. A silhouette of eternal flame. She was beautiful, and she was here. "'M'alright," Leo said in a coarse voice. Her muscles relaxed. "Can I tell you a secret?"

Tate tried to laugh, play along with the ridiculous question, but it came out as a small sob. "Goddammit. What is it, Leo?" she asked, wiping her wet face with a sniffle, and then again brushing Leo's hair and the side of her face with the lightest touch, leaving trails of sparks on her skin. That touch could heal the world.

Leo smiled at the girl kneeling above her. The pain was forgotten for the moment. There was not a fraction of fear or hesitation in Leo's voice when she said it. "I think I'm in love with you."

AFTER

NUMB HANDS RETIED the knot in Leo's hair, a few forgotten fiery strands dangling over her ears and tickling the back of her neck. Alone with her aunt and uncle in what she was beginning to accept as the interrogation room, she kept her eyes glued to the metal table, desperate to avoid either of their gazes and her own glaring back from the two-way mirror covering the wall across from her. She could've sworn she felt the burning of her reflection's stare prickling over her skin. It was probably laughing at her.

Aunt Deborah took the now vacant seat across from Leo and tried to grasp her niece's hands, which promptly jerked out of reach. The woman sighed. She opened her mouth to speak, but Uncle Mike beat her to it. "Leo, you're going to be alright." The soft-spoken man stood next to his wife's chair facing Leo, but his voice sounded far away and lost.

Everyone hesitated at that. Deb looked up at Mike helplessly, but after a second, when she turned back to Leo, her expression changed to one of cautious care, the kind of quiet caution one would use when addressing an unpredictable child or an unstable stranger. Then, in that moment, Leo hated her for it. "We want to help you," Deb said finally. "Please talk to us."

Leo glanced up in a startled confusion, which she tried her best to hide. Her aunt had never pleaded with her like that. The resignation in her tone made Leo uncomfortable.

"What do you want me to say?" It wasn't difficult to ward off the tears stinging the backs of her eyes. To replace the agony with anger. "Tate is still missing. It's been days. And now they think I did something to her. I don't know what I'm supposed to do—this is *insane*—"

"Leo—"

"Let me fucking talk." The table wobbled as she gripped it hard and spat the words with a venom she had never used against her aunt. Mike actually flinched, but Deb held her niece's gaze with cold steadiness. "My girlfriend is *gone,* and I have no idea where she went or what happened to her, and they think I—they think we— you don't *get* it! I love her!"

The little family had never been one to discuss Leo's relationship. The word *love* hung in the air like a curse, but she didn't care.

"Leo." Aunt Deb spoke levelly, but her cheeks began to redden. "I know you loved that girl. It's just that our family has a tendency to . . . overreact?" She looked to Mike for approval on the description, but he just shrugged. "Or, I suppose you could say, spiral." Leo furrowed her brow but didn't break eye contact, curling her hands into fists under the table to hide the tremors. "Your mother felt it too. Hell, she was my little sister; I'm sure you could imagine us growing up together. The fights we had!" Deb broke off into a sad, reminiscent chuckle. "She would know what to do right now, that Ava. But she's not here and I'm all you got. So I need you to be here and listen to me. It's okay. I know you were with that girl the night she disappeared."

You can't even say her name. Leo trembled, her anger now mixing with fear like a spiked drink. That wasn't difficult to deduce; the night had ended with Leo coming home late.

"If you said something to her that night, or did something, I want you to tell me."

All emotion dropped from Leo's face as she stared at her aunt. A calculated wipe that left a pale blank slate in its wake. "You really think I did something?" Her voice was small but blunt. She should have guessed as much. The cagey steps around the house that her aunt had begun to take these past few days Leo had interpreted as an aversion to her niece's grief. Now she wondered if Deb had suspected her involvement all along.

"I don't know, honey." Uncle Mike rubbed Deb's shoulder carefully. A warning.

"I want you to leave," Leo said plainly. Eyes unblinking and absent.

"I—*We're* here to help you." Deb's tone grew more bitter with each word.

"Please go."

Mike murmured something and nudged his wife, who at first wouldn't budge. She screwed up her face in an expression not unlike Leo's. "Fine," she spat. "But don't you come cryin' to me when you get yourself in deeper shit." Deb stomped out of the bland room, the heavy door slamming shut behind her before Mike could follow.

Her uncle paused, and looked at her apologetically. "We left your skateboard at the front desk; couldn't bring it in here but thought it might make you feel better. Just take it home once you're done here. Sebbie's waiting for you at the house." Mike spoke as if she were an uncooperative child getting a shot at the doctor's office, ready to scream at any second. "Your aunt will calm down," he added on his way out the door, the usual band-aid after an outburst. Then he left, and Leo was alone.

➤➤➤➤◄◄◄◄

Warm hands brushed across her ribcage. A smile pressed against a smile. "You're dumb," Tate had said with a mirthless laugh.

"Yeah, well, I'm alive," Leo protested. She was thankful; a few sore spots on her abdomen, which would inevitably bruise, and a couple of scraped elbows were the only injuries sustained in the altercation with Jonathan earlier that day. Once it had been established that Leo wasn't as hurt as it looked, Tate had gingerly walked her inside and washed the dirt and specks of blood off her shirt and the knuckles on her right hand. There was a nervous tenderness with each touch that made Leo feel that delicious sense of surreality and warmth. Couldn't help but remember the two of them caring for Sebago after the dog got hurt in the woods. The effortless sweetness that followed from Tate. Leo rarely allowed anyone to take care of her like this—and certainly not her aunt. Dizzying and electrifying.

It wasn't until Tate was kneeling in front of the other girl and gently rubbing a damp cloth over Leo's knuckles that she addressed the earlier confession. Her voice was a whisper after silence, but a confident one. "I love you too," Tate had said. That's all. Though she was done tending to Leo's sore hand, she kept hold of it and absently played with the bass-callused fingers so much paler and thinner than her own.

Leo guessed this was what it felt like to be drunk.

The pair lay in Tate's bed and stayed there until Tate's mother returned home. The only tangible thoughts in Leo's mind were the feeling of the soft borrowed shirt on her skin and the steady rhythm of someone else's breathing against her side. Nothing could ruin this peace, she thought. She would return to this memory on innumerable occasions, the first time their lips had touched, so cautiously. As if Leo was afraid she would break Tate.

Of course, no one could predict at the time that Jonathan would go home to his parents with a black eye and bloody lip and claim that he'd been attacked.

It was fortunate that Leo and her family weren't charged with anything. But there was now a mark on Leo's record that distinguished her as potentially violent. Dangerous. "I'm not letting you get hurt again. I don't *care* if you thought you were fucking defending her!" Aunt Deb had yelled. Deb made sure to bar any contact that Leo could have had with Tate for the following several weeks of the summer. Leo just nodded and accepted the punishment.

There were ways around it.

Time passed unconsciously in the dull room. It was impossible to guess at the time, having no windows to go by. Leo shifted in her seat. Eventually, she resigned herself to folding her legs up so her chin could rest on her knees, not caring how juvenile the pose felt. She wanted to be small and contained.

This was how she sat when Detective Ander finally returned to the interrogation room, as she was beginning to nod off and surrender to exhaustion. She drew a sharp breath as the metal door screeched open and shook her head to clear away the fog of sleep.

"Hello again, Leo." The detective unceremoniously returned to his original chair across the table. He was noticeably more disheveled than their first interaction; a bead of sweat ran down the side of his face, and his tone took on a more disgruntled connotation. Leo wondered if he'd run into Deb on his way here and wanted to smirk at the thought.

The man still carried the same file that held information about Leo's fight, but it now appeared thicker and was accompanied by a sealed clear bag containing a book. An evidence bag. Bold red lettering declared it as such.

The file was placed intentionally on top of the book, obscuring it from Leo's view. "Sorry for the wait," Detective Ander said, forcing a friendly smile.

"What's that?" Leo asked, stretching her legs. Her voice was careful, gaze trained on the book.

The detective uttered a small laugh then, taking off his thin glasses and rubbing his eyes. "An interesting case, this one," he began. "You see, they called me up here from Boston to investigate a missing persons case. I'm thinking to myself, sure, run-of-the-mill sort of deal. Not certain why they would need my help. This girl probably ran away, and we would find her in a day or two. Nothing the local

PD couldn't handle. The profile fits it, anyway—a young lesbian of color feeling trapped in a tiny hometown. It made sense." Leo tensed. *Tate is bi, asshole.* "But then I started really looking into it. Into both of you."

Leo narrowed her eyes. "So you think because I defended myself against some bigot that I would hurt my girlfriend?"

"You know, I *wouldn't* think that," the detective shrugged, "if there weren't such strange patterns of behavior expressed by the pair of you. You were seen wandering around the town cemetery several times together, most often at night. That's one thing. Maybe you were curious, or looking for a cheap thrill. And a Ouija board, really?" He laughed again. "I can get past that. But I do wonder—why were you two so obsessed with the *woods* beyond the cemetery? Is there something back there?"

Leo's heart dropped. She was beginning to fear the contents of that book. The worst part of it—nausea crept along her abdomen—was that the detective's story was starting to make sense.

The detective continued without waiting for a response. "Marion Mulder—that's Tate's mother, as I'm sure you know—told me that her perfectly happy daughter had changed in the weeks leading up to her disappearance. She was quieter. Paranoid. Then, on the morning of September fifth, Marion went up to Tate's room to wake her up for school. The room was empty, and the window was left open."

The thought of Tate's mom finding a vacant bedroom pained her. "I know," Leo said.

He mumbled his assent, then cleared his throat. The file was moved to the side, exposing the sealed-away book. "Do you recognize this, Leo?" Detective Ander asked. "It was left on Tate's bed. Marion found it."

Leo stared at the book, hoping desperately that she was mistaken. It was impossible. But then the detective opened the evidence bag and placed the well-worn book on the metal table, all crumpled pages and haphazard papers taped inside. The cover was blank, a dark material with imprints of overlapping writing from someone pressing down too hard while they wrote on a long-gone paper on top of it. If the fluorescent lights above caught it the right way, she could make out an 'e' here, a swooping 'y' there. The rest looked like no more than indented scribbles on a previously-pristine fake leather cover.

It was Tate's notebook.

"Well?" The detective prodded, regarding Leo with calculating, focused eyes.

"You shouldn't have that," Leo said without thinking. Her heart pounded against her ribs. It shouldn't have been a surprise that the detective had found the book, but somehow she had pushed it far from her mind. Hadn't *wanted* to think about it.

"Hmm." The man returned his glasses to their accustomed place on his face and flipped through the pages in a way that made Leo's skin crawl. They crinkled with overuse, water damage, and the weight of the taped-in excerpts. She resisted the urge to slap his hands away from it. "This is interesting enough by itself, of course. For the mentions of you alone, considering our situation. And your little adventures with Tate are worth bearing in mind. Seems like it was fun at first. Tate had quite a collection going here. Pretty morbid stuff for two little girls to be exploring." He glanced at Leo over his spectacles. A flare of loathing brought warmth to her cheeks. "But do you know what page this book was open to when Marion found it on her daughter's bed, sans Tate?"

And Leo was afraid that she could guess.

BEFORE

"**DO YOU LIKE** scary stories?"

Leo thought about it. Aisles of books towered over her and Tate as they picked one to wander into, the smell of the pages a nostalgic reverie. The Eston Public Library was small, but hundreds of novels, magazines, and forms of digital entertainment were contained here. It was nearly vacant in the middle of the summer day, only a couple of people working behind the circulation desk when they walked in. Mrs. Annie, a woman who insisted on being addressed with a formal prefix and yet introduced herself by first name only, had been working there long before either of them came to be, and waved a silent hello as they entered. Both Leo and Tate had come here for storytime as kids, but they barely knew each other then, only in passing. It was a strange thought, picturing them in the same room at such a young age. Leo faintly remembered being annoyed at how loud Tate would be while the librarian (often the tired Mrs. Annie) tried in vain to wrangle the group of children and read them a book aloud.

"Depends, I guess. Stephen King's a cool dude," Leo said, realizing that Tate had guided her into the somewhat slim horror section.

"Indeed. How about conspiracies?" Tate grinned, leaning against a thick stack of novels and regarding Leo with a raised eyebrow. The white fluorescent lights above the narrow aisle made her look ghoulish.

Leo tilted her head, amused. "Like faking the moon landing?"

"No—well, I mean, Stanley Kubrick *did*—"

"That was a joke," Leo laughed. "You've been getting more into that stuff lately, huh? Like Bigfoot and the Mothman?"

"Oh, *hell* yeah!" Tate exclaimed, pulling a title from the shelf. *The Shining.* She flipped through the old pages idly. "Well, beyond just them and other cryptids." Leo snickered at her terminology. Tate didn't seem to notice. "They're just some of the better-known ones; there's tons of urban legends out there. Most of which we'll never know because they're so localized. And there's always more to a story than what people tell you, anyway. They're telling you *their* version of it. If you want the truth, you need to find it yourself."

"Hmm." She considered this. The fluorescent library lights left dark imprints on the edges of Leo's vision. "You wouldn't be able to find the truth, though. There would *be* no truth. If a hundred individual people retold one story, the same exact one, then you'd still have a hundred different stories. Infinite urban legends. Makes it so that there is no fact and there is no fiction. Reality becomes subjective."

Tate studied her as she spoke, making Leo overly aware of her mouth. Her subconscious raised a hand to cover the lower part of her face. "Interesting," Tate exhaled. She closed the book with a snap and thought for a moment, tracing the embossed title with a fingertip. "What *is* there, then? If there's no fact and no fiction? There can't just be *nothing*. I'd counter that only means people have the choice to believe whatever they want. For example, you know, God's not real, but some people base their whole lives off trying to appease some dude in the sky who, for some reason, gives a shit about them and their insignificant little lives. They're afraid—terrified—of circumstance, and so they believe in their religion to cope. It becomes part of who they are, it becomes *their* reality, but it's obviously fake. The truth is out there. The *real* truth. We just have to find it at the root of humanity's fear."

Leo considered this. "Fear makes people believe stupid things. Doesn't mean that the thing they're afraid of is real."

Tate smiled, turning her attention from the novel to the girl standing in front of her. "Oh, I think it does." Leo had moved closer without thinking, the smell of Tate's flowery deodorant now mixing with the dusty books. "There's truth behind all fiction, whether you want to see it or not. And fear," Tate tucked a stray strand of hair behind Leo's ear, "is all the proof we need."

The plain statement was greeted with silence from Leo. Fear is all the proof we need.

Tate hugged *The Shining* close to her chest for a moment, then returned the volume to the shoulder-level shelf and wandered away from Leo without another word. Leo stared after her. *This girl may be the death of me*. She then bounded up beside her just before she could turn the corner into another one of the maze-like aisles.

"I think that everyone has something to hide. Not necessarily in a bad way. But sometimes things are better left unspoken, you know?" Tate's expression changed from mischievous to calculating as she once again granted Leo some eye contact.

"Unspoken?" Leo bit her lip, feeling exposed to Tate's stare.

"Mm-hmm." She lowered her gaze then. Even though Tate was only a couple of inches taller than Leo, the gesture made Leo feel very small. Tate leaned her back against the closest bookshelf and pulled Leo closer by the hips. They stared at each other, Tate daring Leo to move and Leo remaining stubbornly still. Their gazes were even and unwavering, despite the pounding in Leo's chest, which she was positive Tate could feel. After an eternity, Tate let go of a breathy giggle and kissed Leo gently on the lips.

The sterile fluorescent light overhead flickered and buzzed. The two broke apart, leaving Leo breathless.

"'You are afraid of me, because I talk like a Sphinx.'"

That playful glint returned to Tate's eyes, and Leo would be lying if she said she wasn't relieved.

"*Jane Eyre,*" Leo identified. "English is the one class I pay attention to, Tate. Your references aren't lost on me."

"Well, they were lost on Jonathan, so I'm glad you caught it."

"Hah. I'm not afraid of you." The fading bruises on her knuckles seemed to tingle. That hand found its way to the small of Tate's back and then her hip. "What's gotten into you today? Why did you want to go to the library?"

"I can't be in a literary mood?" Tate curled her fingers around Leo's wrist like a cuff and started walking through the aisles again.

Leo had promised Aunt Deb she was going to the library alone, and the woman assented, but the look in her eyes as she stepped out the door was one of quiet suspicion. Leo couldn't help glancing over her shoulder periodically, positive that Deb would appear any moment from behind a stack of books and catch her with Tate. Which was ridiculous; Leo could do whatever she wanted. And she wanted to be with Tate. "Follow me. But promise you won't think I'm weird for this," Tate said.

"Bit late for that." Leo smirked, but allowed the other girl to pull her forward and followed into a different towering aisle.

Tate brought her over to the local history section of the library and pulled a chair out at one of the wooden tables for Leo to sit in. "Stay here a second," she said, then disappeared between the narrow rows of shelves.

Leo yawned as she sat down and readjusted the knot in her hair. It wasn't unusual for Tate to act so purposefully strange for the fun of it, but Leo wanted an explanation this time, and she thought she might be lucky enough to get one today.

When Tate reemerged a couple of minutes later, her arms were full of several different volumes varying in lengths and subjects, the stack stretching from her torso up to her nose. The tower of books toppled over as soon as she reached the table, and Leo reached her arms out so none would fall to the floor with what she was sure would be a sound like a gunshot in the silence of the library.

Unexplained Phenomena. A Beginner's Guide to the Occult. Wicca, Women, and New England Folktales. Field Reports: American UFOs. Applied Anthropology. The Truth about Urban Legends. These were just a few of the titles laid out before Leo.

She paused, scanning over the bountiful books. "Interesting," Leo echoed, unsure of the response Tate wanted. "You've checked all these out, then?"

"Yep. But there's more." Tate pointed to a smaller book, partially hidden under a thicker volume. *A Practical Study of Crows: Their Prominence and Symbolism.* And another, nearby: *Woodland Wonders.*

" . . . Okay? What about them?" Leo looked up at Tate, who was still standing and leaning over the books.

Tate handed Leo one of them then, a withered paperback that was falling apart at the seams. *The Other History of Maine.* "Weird things happen sometimes," Tate said.

Leo flicked her gaze over all the books, repeatedly finding titles she hadn't noticed at first glance. She pulled at one of her fair eyebrows, thinking. "This is the research you mentioned? You believe all this?"

Tate's eagerness deflated. "Well, I mean, not *all* of it. But there's something here. I know there is. I'll show you later. I have a whole notebook full of stuff—urban legends especially—it makes *sense* that some of it is true. Some of it *has* to be. Like, for example, you ever heard of black dogs?"

Leo shook her head, and Tate retrieved a small volume from beneath a few other books on the table, flipping through yellowed pages until she landed on a darkened sketch.

"It's an extraordinary legend. They're these huge dogs

with glowing eyes that come at night. People have described them as specters, demons, apparitions, pretty much every name in the book. Some are shapeshifters! It's said that if you see one, you're destined to die. They're portents of death," she said, voice climbing a wave of intensity. Leo shrunk back by degrees. "Best part is, they're not all so sinister. There have been a few documented cases in New England where a huge ghostly dog purportedly guided lost hikers back onto the right forest paths at night. Some guarded campsites from bigger dangers. All these monsters and urban legends—they're not all something to fear. It's *amazing*. Multiple reports of this, Leo. I want to know about all those old campfire stories that scare people. I want to know the truths behind them."

Their voices had carried across the library more than they realized, and Leo stifled a laugh as Mrs. Annie, working behind the main desk, averted her stare and tried to appear busy shuffling some papers as soon as Leo happened to glance up. Tate waited tensely, and Leo wanted to surrender to her logic. She really did. *I trust you, but . . . why?* "I don't know, dude," Leo leaned back in the creaky chair. It hurt to see Tate disappointed. So she amended her disbelief with a crooked but amused smile. "Sometimes things just happen, and we don't understand them. Doesn't matter how weird they seem. There are rational explanations. Those hikers probably saw a coyote or something."

"Come on. There are so many cases like that. Don't go skeptic on me now, love." Tate sat down across from Leo, the second wooden chair squeaking beneath her. It felt suddenly as if Leo was being questioned by Tate, but somehow, she didn't mind. Couldn't even if she tried. So she would play along. Tate's words were teasing, coming out of a venomous smirk. She held Leo's hand. Ran a thumb over the old bruises still discoloring her pale knuckles. Then, softly, "I want to do something. Tonight. And I need your help."

Leo risked a grin sparked by the danger in Tate's tone. "We going Bigfoot hunting?"

She lifted Leo's hand from the table and brushed her mouth across the fading bruises without breaking eye contact. When she spoke, her full lips tickled Leo's skin. "Oh, no. Something much more fun."

AFTER

AVA BATES WAS a determined woman who lived with purpose in every fiber of her being. Leo's conception had admittedly been the one unplanned action she ever took, as Ava and Kenneth had barely broken 21 before Ava had gotten pregnant, and as yet unmarried, they decided that their daughter would take Ava's surname. They never ended up getting married, actually—the couple often spoke of a wedding in a dreamy way; perhaps they would tie the knot when baby Leo was older and could play a bigger role in the ceremony, or maybe when each of their families finally warmed up to the other. Ava hardly minded. She dedicated her life to her daughter, and Kenneth loved her deeply. Leo couldn't recall a single time her mother had raised her voice at her. It was almost inconceivable that Ava and Deborah were sisters; where Deb was fueled by frustration and self-righteousness, Ava ran in pursuit of bliss and contentment. There was an old photograph that Leo liked to keep in her wallet of her mother, fiery hair identical to her own flowing in the wind and covering her eyes as she smiled over her shoulder in the direction of a younger Leo pointing a cheap disposable camera. It was Leo's favorite picture. Her mother was so *happy,* so in love, but with a quiet sort of sobriety that kept her hands folded and her shoulders stiff. Ice that sunk deep inside her and splintered there instead of floating to the surface and freezing all it touched. Everything Ava did was purposeful and conscious.

Killing herself and Kenneth had ripped that photo to shreds.

Leo, then ten years old, was woken for school by her mother just like any other day. The morning was so ordinary and monotonous that Leo barely remembered any details about it, couldn't say if anything was off between her parents. Kenneth had made her breakfast as usual; she gave each of them a grumpy kiss goodbye and left for class.

When Leo stepped off the bus in her parents' driveway later that afternoon and there was no one waiting to meet her there, she was a bit disappointed but still didn't sense anything wrong. The house was cleaner than usual; all the dishes clean and clothes folded, and floors vacuumed. "Mom?" Leo called from the entryway as she kicked off her Chucks. No response. Kenneth would still be at work, and Ava likely went out to do some errands. They would be back soon. Nothing was wrong.

It happened in the woods. Probably not long after Leo had left for school that morning.

She remembered the police knocking on her door just as the twilight was setting in. The dark had settled around her in the vacant house as she awaited her parents' return and hadn't bothered to turn the lights on. An unsteady silence lingered about her shoulders as she stared at the window across the room. It was one of those silences that is so penetrating and chasmic that after a few hours, you start to hear a ringing, then that ringing morphs into whispers, and the whispers might be saying your name, over and over, and then they scream. Leo didn't remember moving from the couch to the floor, but she found herself sitting cross-legged in the middle of the living room, hardly feeling the worn carpet beneath her, entranced by the quiet and swallowed whole. A century may have passed before the urgent *tap-tap-tap* on her door cut through the shadows like a spray of bullets. Startled out of the daze, she drifted like a phantom to the front door. Standing on tiptoes, shifting the curtains aside just a few inches and peeking through the window. Leo saw the flashing red and blue lights cascading over her own reflected face, and did not cry.

Policemen had streamed into the house after she opened the door wordlessly and turned on the lights, stinging her eyes, to search all the rooms for any clue or motivation. What had previously been that horrible silence in Leo's ears was now a deafening shuffle of unknown bodies and solemn voices. The cop who had been the one designated to tell Leo of the tragedy tried his best to be delicate, but the delivery felt pitiful even to the ten-year-old. He knelt in front of where she sat motionless on the couch. "Hi there, Leonora. Why didn't you call someone when your parents weren't home?"

"They're coming back soon," she said.

The man sighed and rubbed a hand through his stubble. Wouldn't look her in the eyes. "I'm so sorry, but no, they're not, dear."

Ava Bates had taken a Swiss Army knife she'd had since she was a teenager, led her partner into the woods a mile or so behind their house, closer to the road on the other side, which was technically across the town line, without a single sign of struggle from Kenneth, and vertically slit both of their wrists. The papers said their blood covered the bed of leaves they rested upon, Ava cradling Kenneth's head in her lap as she leaned her back limply against a tree. She'd cut his first, then her own. Her head had lolled forward in death, strands of fiery hair shrouding her face and dangling over her partner's, standing out angrily against the disturbing paleness of both. The bodies were found by an old man who'd stopped his car on the road nearby to take a piss in the woods.

Obviously, the cop didn't tell her the gruesome truth upfront. She'd gotten that from other sources. He just said they were gone, then waited patiently for her response.

Young Leo took the kitchen knife she'd been hiding

under her favorite *Alien* shirt and buried it up to the handle in the cop's shoulder.

"I don't want to talk anymore."

Detective Ander cleared his throat, flipping through Tate's notebook until he reached a specific page. That page. Leo knew without needing to look. The coldness of the metal chair she was sitting on did nothing to ease the tension in her shoulders. "So your parents died in a murder-suicide," the man said, taking no heed of Leo's objection. "That doesn't seem to fit with a lot of the other things Miss Mulder has collected here. Everything else is all conspiracies, the occasional bizarre crime, cold cases—things that could be argued to be, well, *unexplainable*, is the term Tate often used," the detective said. "But the deaths of Ava and Kenneth are perfectly explainable. The case was closed almost immediately. Your mother was ill, and that was essentially all there was to it. So why stick this in there?"

He spun the book around so that Leo could read it right-side up. Of course it was open to the spread of newspaper clippings describing her parents' deaths. There were a couple of pictures of the scene, too—the mostly-obscured image that had been printed in the papers on one side of the spread and more graphic crime scene photos on the other side that Leo couldn't look at. She never got the answer to where and how Tate had gotten the pictures. More notes in Tate's flowing handwriting hung in the margins like lace. Leo didn't want to read them. The red ink of her scribbled notes brought a metallic taste to Leo's mouth.

An unsteady hand reached forward and lifted the page, half expecting the paper to burn her skin. After the spread with her parents, there were a few more notes in red ink, and among them, Leo's name appeared more than once. But what Leo really needed to see was in the middle of these pages. Ripped edges near the binding. A couple of the pages had been torn out. She quickly molded her expression into one of unaffected neutrality and flipped back to her parents' grisly pages.

"It just doesn't make sense to me," Detective Ander went on after Leo remained silent. She hoped he regarded the lost pages as merely further demonstration of Tate's paranoia. Hoped he wouldn't go looking for them. "And then that along with these expunged court records I found. It's a puzzling situation, even for me."

At this point, Leo was hardly surprised. There's only one thing he could be talking about. She pinched the skin of her inner forearms. "That cop forgave me. He was fine after. My parents had just fucking died, and I wasn't thinking."

"I know; that's why it was expunged. Cataloged as an accident. Very charitable of that guy. But a ten-year-old girl stabbing a policeman with a knife is hardly something to be overlooked in our case, Leo. I'm sure you understand that."

She'd just caught the guy off guard, that's all. Was so spaced out and upset at the news that without a sound, she moved her thin arm swiftly and sunk the knife in, felt it caress against his collarbone. Watched herself do it from afar as if in a dream. She wasn't sure when she had taken that knife from the kitchen. Must have been when she was waiting in the dark. It might have poked out the other side of the cop; the knife was that big. A carving knife, or whatever. Though she couldn't see it from where the other officers had converged to yank her away and restrain her. She didn't remember fighting, didn't even try to speak. Blood blossomed from the cop's shoulder like a wilting rose and skimmed the side of Leo's childish hand, but she wasn't scared. Only empty. The widened eyes of the wounded cop revealed that he was, though.

That look, the one of horror and astonishment that the towering cop had given in response to a girl of her size and age, brought a ridiculous smirk to Leo's face now.

"Something funny?" Detective Ander hardened his expression from across the interrogation table. He watched her over his spectacles.

Her smile was venomous, but she tried to swallow against her hatred for the man. In the face of condemnation, she would feign arrogance. "You keep trying to link all these things together, but you have absolutely no idea what you're talking about. I think that's pretty damn funny." Leo willed herself to adopt a nonchalant demeanor. Something she did often in school after her parents passed away. She leaned back in her chair to take a breath and met his gaze evenly.

"So why don't you fill me in, huh?" He took the notebook and closed it with a soft thud. Leo felt as though he just screwed the lid back onto a jar full of wailing ghosts. The heaviness of expectation settled in the windowless room. Detective Ander folded his hands to hold up his chin on the table and studied her.

"My past is irrelevant to Tate. She was interested in it, that's all. She's always into weird stuff like that. The fact that my mom was sick doesn't mean I am, and doesn't mean I hurt my girlfriend. It doesn't mean anything was Mom's fault, either. You're the sickest one in this room if you think I would do *anything* to hurt Tate. I love her, and I'm waiting for her to come home, and here you are wasting your time questioning me when she could be in actual trouble out there. Please, *please*, find her." Leo loathed herself for begging, but didn't try to stop the words from escaping her lips. Her eyes stung, but she fought the tears back. She would not cry.

Detective Ander took her words under consideration. His chair creaked as he leaned back, a mirror of Leo's posture, and let out a deep breath. The dark eyes shifted from Tate's notebook to Leo and back again. Then, finally, he responded. "I can tell you love her," he said. "We're doing everything we can to find her, Leo. You're just going to have to trust that." He stood up, and Leo noticed the sweat stains darkening the fabric under his arms. The chair screeched against the linoleum as he pushed it back. "I'm sending you home for now. I need you to come back here tomorrow, though, and ask the front desk for me. We have more to discuss. Can I trust you to do that? I'll send someone to get you again if I can't. Not an issue."

Relief flooded Leo's face with a warmth she could feel. "You can trust me," she said, standing up without breaking eye contact. And he *would* trust her.

"Alright." The detective slipped the withered notebook back into the transparent red evidence bag. Leo's gaze followed his fingers as they zipped it up. He held out a massive hand, and Leo gripped it in a firm handshake across the table. Without letting her go, he pulled her arm in a little closer and spoke in a softer voice. She shrunk from the scent of his cigarette-breath. They must have been talking for hours, and he still reeked of it. "I'm on your side, Leo. I don't want to find you at the end of this. I truly don't."

Leo actually believed him. She let go of his hand and took a step back, legs stiff from sitting for so long. Her eyes were hard, unblinking. "You won't."

The man followed her out of the interrogation room and to the lobby of the police station, where she was able to pick up her skateboard from the front desk. Had it really been just that afternoon when Aunt Deb and Uncle Mike had come? Eons had passed in this building. The man behind the desk eyed Leo as he handed her the skateboard and kept watching as she said her uneasy goodbye to Detective Ander. Night had dropped its curtain early with that uniquely-September wistfulness. She walked out of the station and inhaled as if she'd been suffocating, the cold making her lungs ache. All was blue-dark with pinpricks of stars poking through the trees above and the occasional pair of headlights blazing by on the road. Dangerous to be skating, especially with the rain from earlier that day, but she didn't care. Out from that place, the tears came back, and Leo didn't stop them. Those ripped-out pages . . . she needed to get them. God *damn* it, Tate. Resisted the urge to scream. Her skateboard hit the ground, and she stepped on with a choked sob and skated away, feeling both sets of the men's eyes following her into the dark.

BEFORE

SOMEHOW IT DIDN'T surprise Leo when Tate pulled a Ouija board and planchette out of the trunk of her old Nissan. At her amused look, Tate winked. "Never underestimate my commitment to the craft, baby," she said. The trunk slammed shut after Tate gathered a beat-up notebook from underneath a blanket. She proudly held the book up on display for Leo to see. It was bound in a black leather cover, cracked and softened at the edges. The spine was swollen, and the corners of some pages were sticking out of the sides. "I want you to look through this on our walk over there. Stick to the first few pages," Tate told her. Leo nodded, wondering how far this new hobby of hers was going to go tonight. The board, planchette, two flashlights, and a couple of small candles with a lighter disappeared into a drawstring bag that Tate slung over her shoulders.

"Hold on," Leo held the notebook under her arm as she reached into the pocket of her oversized denim jacket. She stuffed the almost-full pack of cigarettes into Tate's bag. "Alright, now let's go."

"Ooh, so naughty, Leo," Tate teased with a quick peck on her faintly freckled cheek.

"Found 'em in a drawer. My uncle hasn't smoked in a while, so I figured he wouldn't miss them. Probably be glad they're gone."

"True. Fits the mood, too." The fading sunlight cast an orange glow across Tate's cheekbones as they started their walk into the cemetery.

Dead leaves crunched below their sneakers, the pavement turning into a dirt path down the middle of the gravestones. Cars whooshed by from the road behind them, causing strange howls to drift through the air. Leo cradled Tate's notebook in her arms—it was a hefty thing, with papers taped into certain pages making it bulge at the seams. She lifted open the cover. *Tate Mulder,* it read in her scrawling handwriting, *Uncanny Archive.* "Is this a story you wrote or something?" Leo asked.

"Nope," Tate said through a grin. "Call it a history project." She took out a cigarette and lit it with a flick as it dangled from her lips, sheltering the lighter's small flame from the breeze.

Leo knit her brows and glanced at Tate sideways but flipped to the first page without comment. A newspaper headline from the *Portland Press Herald* was paper-clipped in: NO LEADS ON MISSING CHILDREN CASE. From 1994. Then, underneath the headline, Tate's stringy letters hung in bullet points. Something about the woods outside a kid's house. Leo kept Tate in her periphery as they walked, her trailing slightly behind, and tried to pay more attention to the notebook than the way the girl's fingers delicately held the cigarette.

According to Tate's notes, a family's dog had been found mangled and killed by an unidentified animal just a few feet into the underbrush before the kid had gone missing. Leo shuddered and turned to the next page. No headline, just a spread filled top to bottom with notes from Tate. And a hand-drawn map of the Eston cemetery, an arrow pointing down to where the turnpike exit would be, little uneven mounds showing a few gravestones, and an asterisk by the edge of the trees beyond the graves indicating some kind of "Entrance." Another page had pictures taped in, presumably taken by Tate herself, where an out-of-focus blur across the daytime sky was circled in red marker and another of a thick wood with two orbs of yellow light gleaming from the distance. More headlines and articles from as far back as the eighties were attached to the pages Leo flipped through. ESTON MAN FALLS OFF BRIDGE ONTO RUSH-HOUR TURNPIKE. ALL PETS GO MISSING IN NEIGHBORHOOD. ATTEMPTED ARMED ROBBERY ENDS IN BURGLAR SCREAMING FOR HELP, SENT TO AUGUSTA MENTAL HEALTH INSTITUTE. REPORTS OF UNIDENTIFIED MAN IN ESTON WOODS INCREASE. There were photocopied selections from a few of the library books she'd shown Leo earlier that day collected inside, and more she didn't recognize. Unsolved true crime stories in New England, a paragraph about the Salem witch trials, UFO sightings, and part of an essay with a thesis explaining the societal implications of urban legends.

"Tate, what are these?" Leo felt Tate's gaze on her as she flipped through the rest of the notebook in a blur, slightly concerned about what else may lie between the pages.

Smoke strayed from her mouth with the single word. "Evidence." She held out her hands, and Leo stared at them before returning the book. She stuffed her own into her pockets. "You asked me back at the library if I actually believed in all that weird shit I was showing you. In all those books about myths and legends. A lot of that is fake, if I'm honest. But some of it has merit, and that's what I have here. *This* is the shit I believe in." Her fingers tapped the hardback cover, and she hugged the volume close to her chest.

Their feet crunched the dirt path beneath them, the light of day now almost completely faded out to the cool blue-gray hue of dusk, like a filter on a camera. Leo was more confused than ever but said nothing. Today was the first day in a little over a week she had spent with her girlfriend as a result of Aunt Deb's heightened hovering—there was no way she was going to question her.

Tate soon broke the silence again. "I really appreciate you coming out here with me." They had reached the edge of the woods, just past the last row of gravestones and about half a mile or so from the busy road and Tate's parked car. The sound of cars driving by had died out to a soft wail. "You probably hate coming here. I promise it'll be worth your while."

"Why would I hate coming to the cemetery?" It may have been cruel of her to set that trap for Tate, but she asked the question anyway.

Tate tilted her head. "Well, your parents are here, aren't they?" She paused, seemingly reconsidering the response. "Sorry."

"No, don't apologize." Not angry, just saying. She cleared her throat and walked a few paces before speaking up again. "That still doesn't exactly clear anything up for me, though. Why are we here? I thought you and the woods had a bad history."

Tate's shoulders relaxed, and she giggled. "Guess I'm getting braver." She turned to kiss Leo's cheek, sending shivers down her spine, then stepped beyond the treeline with the drawstring bag of odd supplies swinging against her back. Before she could disappear into the shadow of the woods, Leo hurried up to follow.

⟫⟫⟫⟪⟪⟪

The woods beyond the Eston cemetery were not the kind meant for wandering. Darkness leeched down from the sky through the splintered tree branches above, running like spilled ink to the leaves below. Two flashlights illuminated a few paces ahead of Leo and Tate, small breaks in the shadows that betrayed the former's uncertainty with each step.

Tate had said that the walk would be short. In truth, as the sun set behind them, it felt more like an off-path hike. One that is meant to be traveled in a straight line and is linear at the ground level. However, if Leo could have seen their path from a bird's eye view, she wouldn't be surprised if they'd taken unplanned turns or started going around in circles. Everywhere looked the same, flashlight-illuminated trees and only Tate's back and bright red sneakers to break up the scene in front of Leo. She found herself reaching for the handle of Tate's drawstring backpack as they ambled to an unspecified destination.

After some time that Leo was sure should have brought them out the far side of the woods, all the way to the paved bypass road that would eventually reach the high school, they stopped their walk amongst the trees. A gnarled stone frame sat comfortably on the side of a hill, laced with mosses and lichens. An iron ring hung as a rusted handle from the weathered boards of a door. Leo had never seen this place—never ventured out this far past the gravestones.

"What is this?" Leo's flashlight traced the perimeter of the door.

"We're gonna figure that out tonight." Tate tapped the ashes from her cigarette, which was down to the filter. She put down her flashlight and pulled the iron ring a few times, leaning back with all her might, and the door didn't budge. Didn't make a sound at all besides the metal clang of the handle as she dropped it back, and it hit the door. Dead and vacant. She huffed. "I have some theories."

Tate opened her bag and rummaged through her supplies, flashlight resting on a small stone nearby to light her way. Leo lowered herself beside her, eyes on the door cautiously. It was strange. She felt as though the temperature had dropped twenty degrees since they'd stepped into the vicinity of this old door.

"There's only one or two mentions of this door in any of the things I've read about Eston," Tate said while she worked. "They call it an 'entrance,' but they never say anything else about it. I mentioned it in a few pages in my notebook; you probably saw. You'd think maybe it's some kind of underground access to the cemetery—to the crypts, or whatever, if that's a thing that cemeteries still do—but then wouldn't there be more information on it? Wouldn't it look less abandoned? Something about it bothers me. And the fact that it's in the middle of the woods, at least a mile from the last few gravestones. The woods are strange here, as you and I both know. Maybe this is, like . . . the source."

"There's no way we're only a mile out. We were walking forever."

"Mm-hmm. We certainly were." Leo didn't have to look at Tate to know that she was amused.

She scoffed. "Whatever. I think you just got us lost." The Ouija board and planchette were placed on the ground between them. Leo kept her flashlight on them while Tate set up a few small candles on either side so that the girls themselves completed their circle around the board. As the last candle was lit with the flick of the lighter, Leo pulled a cigarette out of the carton and touched its end to the little wick. She saw Tate smirk as she took a puff. Couldn't help but grin in return. Smoke billowed from her mouth and nose.

"See? This is fun, right?" Tate asked, the candles casting a ghoulish orange glow up her face. Leo figured she must look just as wild as the candlelight caught her smoke. The two sat on the ground with the Ouija board between them and the withered door framed by stone to Leo's right, Tate's left. Tate turned her flashlight off, but Leo kept hers shining from her lap.

"Feels kinda funny." She'd be lying if she said she didn't want to be here with Tate. But all the same, there was a certain prickling along the back of her neck that wouldn't go away.

"Good. It should." Tate placed both her hands on the planchette, then peered up at Leo. "Come on, you too."

Leo sighed and balanced the cigarette loosely between her lips, freeing both hands to join Tate's on the planchette. And waited.

"Nothing's happening," she said, cigarette bouncing a little with her words.

Tate laughed. "We haven't *started,* babe. Just wanna make sure you know the rules. No taking your hands off once we start; it's dangerous when it's not anchored anymore," she said. "We both have to say goodbye when we're done. And obviously, no moving it on purpose. Now we have to say hello first."

"Okay. 'Sup, ghosts, I'm Leo, this is Tate, nice to meet y—"

"Not like that!" Tate cackled. The sound of her laughter was sweet and familiar; a much-needed reassurance. Though it did feel slightly out of place within such a gloomy setting as this. She just didn't want Tate to be too disappointed when they didn't make contact with anything; at least they'd have somewhat of a good time together. The fact that her girlfriend was taking this little séance so seriously made her uneasy, but Leo would humor her for now.

Tate slid the planchette in a couple of slow circles around the board over all its letters and numbers, making Leo's hands follow loyally. It moved with little exertion. Then Tate spoke. "Hello. Is anyone here with us tonight?"

They waited. The planchette remained frozen near the center of the alphabet on no particular letter. Half of the *T* was magnified through the glass orb in the center of the planchette's peak, accompanied by the tail of an *S*. That space in between letters felt chasmic. Nothing. "Are we alone?" Not the slightest movement. Tate furrowed her brow, a headache-inducing habit picked up from spending so much time with Leo. "Why is this door here?"

Motionless silence. Tate let out a grunt of frustration that made Leo smirk. "Fine, you ask, then," Tate said.

"Maybe they're just shy," Leo said. She took a nonchalant, handless drag from the cigarette still dangling between her lips. The smoke came out to underline her somewhat-stifled question. "What do you want me to ask?"

"About the door. It shouldn't be here; there's nowhere for it to go."

"Okay." Leo concentrated. At this point, she wanted *something,* some kind of answer, so Tate wouldn't be upset. She considered moving the planchette herself, but she was a horrible liar. Better for Tate to be let down by her morbid fascination than by her girlfriend. "Uh, if anyone is listening," she began, "Tate wants to know about this door. Where does it lead?"

Nothing, again. She tried to think of something to say that would make Tate feel better and tried to ignore the midnight forest cold seeping through her sweatshirt. Then one of the candles next to her sizzled out. Leo tilted her head. It was a little windy. "Where does this door lead to?" Leo repeated, glancing up to see Tate's widened eyes.

The planchette started gliding. Slowly, almost imperceptibly, but moving. "Tate, you said no moving it yourself," Leo complained.

"I'm not doing that," Tate said, fixated. There was no sound at all—the natural rustling of leaves around them seemed to have gone still. The piece reached the letter *W* and magnified it through the convex glass. There was no fear and hardly any surprise in Tate's expression, which honestly did contribute to Leo's theory that she was just moving it herself. Oh well. She's played along this far; no turning back now. Could be a fun story to tell someday, at least.

Their hands made a sharp turn that surprised Leo and almost made her fingers slip off the planchette. It settled on *H.* Both girls remained silent. Then finally, *O.*

"'Who'?" Tate said. *Who does it lead to, or who are we?* She bit her lip. "Um. I'm Tate Mulder." She looked to Leo, nodding at the board.

"Oh, sorry," she said after a hesitation. Having reached the filter already with all the talking and unanticipated development, Leo spit the butt of her cigarette to the side. Its remaining ashes fizzled out amongst the dead leaves. Her heart pounded, but her voice was unwavering. "I'm Leo. Leo Bates."

The planchette started twitching beneath their fingertips. Leo looked at Tate in confusion and saw her anxious face illuminated by the remaining candles. This wasn't something she was making it do, Leo realized. It wasn't heading in any specific direction on the Ouija board. More like it was testing its force. A sudden gust then blew out the orange candlelight like a breath and whipped their hair in the direction of the door. The planchette vibrated fiercely beneath their fingertips, and they found themselves pressing down harder on the piece to keep it in contact with the board. Leo's flashlight sputtered out and died, and the wind vanished as abruptly as it had come. The darkness swallowed them whole; neither girl could see the other.

Before either could speak, the planchette flew out from beneath both their hands and threw itself against the center of the old door with a loud *wham*. Leo yelped and jumped back. They heard the rounded wooden triangle then fall to the leaf-covered ground, lifeless.

"Tate," Leo said in a low voice. "I thought you said it was dangerous to let go of the—"

She was broken off by the sound of Tate's footsteps running in the direction of the door. "Wait!" Leo bounded up after her, hitting her flashlight a few times until it flickered back to life and revealed Tate holding the teardrop-shaped object, whose cloudy glass orb in the center of the peak was now cracked down the middle. It reflected a warped light back into Leo's eyes, and she winced.

"Oh, god," Tate said, brushing a tangled curl of hair out of her face. "I-I don't know what to do now."

Time to end this stupid game. Leo was beginning to feel sick. "It's okay," she whispered with a hand on Tate's arm, "We'll go say goodbye with the board like you wanted to and then go home. We're okay."

Tate said nothing and studied the door in front of them. She reached for the rusted iron handle with a shaking hand. Leo started and clasped the flashlight tighter. "Hey, I don't think we should—"

The door opened under her touch with a screech, and all hell broke loose.

Air rushed into the ajar doorway like a vacuum, a high-pitched wail. As if the air from the woods around them was busting out of an air-locked jar and into space. There was hardly more than a few inches of open space between the door and its frame, but that didn't matter. It didn't stop. Leaves flew up from the ground and were sucked into the darkness. Leo grabbed Tate's shoulder where she seemed frozen in place to keep from losing her balance and falling too close to it. The sound of rushing wind was all-encompassing and deafening. The few extinguished candles rolled and tumbled toward the opening and disappeared inside, the gale growing stronger. Tate stared into the gap, eyes wide and jaw slack in terror. Not the slightest acknowledgment of Leo trying to pull her away. The spindlier of the trees around them buckled in the direction of the doorway. Branches and thin trunks snapped. The debris whipped the skin of her arms, her face. Tate was unresponsive to Leo's panic. She remained a statue in front of the void.

Seeing her efforts with Tate were futile, Leo turned her attention to the door, and pushed as hard as she could against it, rough crevices in the old wood digging into her palms. It didn't budge as the wind heedlessly flew inside. Next was the Ouija board. It lept into the air and hit the gap in the door with a deafening *crack*, breaking into splinters that were each sucked into it. One of the larger dagger-like splinters cut Leo in the back of her hand where it held the edge of the door. She screamed with the exertion and sudden pain, the sound lost amidst the rushing wind.

Tate's notebook, heavier than the other objects, started being pulled slowly by the force behind the door. Leo pressed her body weight against the withered wood and iron, feeling her muscles wield more power than they contained and tearing, straining, to latch it shut. The wind had dislodged the planchette from Tate's hands and flung it inside. It hit something with an echo that sounded miles away. The vacuum was growing, the door opening wider and wider.

"*Tate,*" Leo almost growled over the gust. Tate was transfixed on the open gap in the door, paralyzed. Her eyes were distant and glazed. The brown irises were beginning to cloud over and turn white. And she was being pulled closer, without her feet taking a single step. Ever so slightly, Tate hovered into the dark, a heavier dark than that of the cemetery woods surrounding them, a dark that the flashlight could not pierce and that Leo's eyes refused to adjust to. "*Close the fucking door!*"

She looked at her as if in a trance, illuminated by the flashlight trapped between Leo and the door. Her stare was deathlike. No pupils or irises. A blank canvas of terrifying white. Leo's heart skipped and she paled. The notebook was a few inches away from the shadowed opening now and fluttered open with the gust. Its pages flipped over themselves as if being skimmed by a frantic apparition.

Tate lifted her hand and pressed it against the door. She seemed to use no strength at all. It slammed shut. The vibration caused the door's rocky frame to crumble and seal it with an unforgiving roar.

Leo fell backward to escape the falling rock and wheezed for breath among the floating dust and debris. Her ears rang; she struggled to stay focused. When she looked up, Tate was standing, breathing in quick gasps like she had been running. "Tate," Leo choked. Her eyes were back to their normal golden brown; the ghostly all-white stare was gone without a trace. Leo must have imagined it—she *must* have.

She stumbled up and enveloped Tate in her arms, resting Tate's head on her shoulder and caressing her hair. Careful not to smear any of the blood from where the splintered Ouija board had struck her hand. The response she got was Tate grasping the back of Leo's sweatshirt like she was the only thing anchoring her to earth. Tate was icy cold; Leo's skin turned red where she had buried her tear-streaked face in Leo's neck. Leo was left reeling after whatever had just happened, but she swallowed her panic for the moment and focused on Tate, both their hearts pounding against their ribs as if trying to get at each other. All they could do was hold each other in the gloom.

Unintelligible words were mumbled against Leo's body. She rubbed Tate's back. "What?"

"Love you," Tate stuttered.

"I love you too." She kissed her temple.

A crow cawed above their heads somewhere in the darkness of the forest, making them both jump. Leo took a deep breath. "We're both okay. Let's go home, yeah?" She gently let go of Tate, who took a small step back after a moment, but lingered a hand on Leo's arm.

"You're bleeding," Tate whispered, staring at the back of her hand.

"I'm okay." Seemed to be the only thing she could say, whether it was true or not. The flashlight she had forgotten she dropped flickered, and she bent down to pick it up distrustfully. Its yellowish light caught the open pages of Tate's notebook, which was somehow more disheveled than before. Leo almost closed the book before she saw the contents of the exposed two-page spread. Another newspaper clipping like the others she'd seen on earlier pages, but this was one she recognized:

TWO ESTON RESIDENTS FOUND DEAD IN MURDER-SUICIDE—LEAVING BEHIND YOUNG DAUGHTER.

There was the picture that had been included in the *Press Herald* article showing Ava and Kenneth's bodies, the gore politely obscured by the forest the couple was found in, framed by caution tape and cops on the scene. Their positions in death were barely discernible. Kenneth's head lay upon Ava's lap as if asleep, and Ava leaned against a tree and slouched lifelessly to the side. Her hand rested in the man's hair. Many times Leo had had nightmares of her mother's blood dripping down from her slashed wrists into her father's paper-white face. Of course, the newspaper picture did not feature such disturbing images. But the full-color crime scene photos taped onto the adjacent page of Tate's notebook depicted just that. Close-ups of the bloody carnage followed by each of her parents' slack faces, Kenneth's dressed in the blood of her mother. And below it all, a picture of ten-year-old Leo, red-faced and mid-scream like a demon being held back by several police officers. Her hands were bloody, the knife she'd used to stab the cop discarded on the carpet before her. Her face was deranged and full of horror, unrecognizable.

Leo collapsed to her knees in front of the book, falling out of Tate's nervous grasp. She wanted to vomit. "Wh-why . . . "

As Tate's dazed stare settled on the open notebook and identified the pages, her eyes widened. "Leo," she began, crouching down beside her. "I was just curious—"

"This is my fucking life!" Leo snapped. She shone the flashlight in Tate's face, who winced with the brightness. The light reflected off the half-dried tears down her cheeks, little streams of silver against the ochre of her skin. Leo's head ached, and the world spun around her. "This isn't some of your urban legend bullshit or a conspiracy! This really happened! My mom killed my dad and then herself, and that's it. There's nothing debatable or *unexplainable* about it, Tate. Why do you have this? How did you even get these pictures?"

"I'm sorry," Tate whispered. "It's just . . . it happened in the woods, and—"

"And you're scared of the woods. I know! But you can't bring my family into this obsession you have with weird shit. You can't bring *me* into it. We're leaving. Come on." Leo's pulse thudded like a feral animal, but she forced her voice to soften. She slapped the notebook shut and looked around for the drawstring bag they'd brought, avoiding both Tate's stare and the now-dilapidated door with its fallen stony frame. The bag must have been sucked into that damn void behind the door—no, she'd just misplaced it. There was no vacuous space, and everything was fine and normal. She pulled at her hair in frustration.

"You *know* the woods are weird; you feel it too. There's something wrong here. You just don't want to see it. You never have," Tate said. "That door—"

"Shut up." Warmth rushed to Leo's face as fresh tears carved streams down Tate's cheeks again. She'd never spoken to Tate this way. Her hurt expression cut through Leo's anger like a blade and created space for the guilt to flood in. That characteristic scowl remained, all the same.

Tate sniffled, then lunged forward and snatched the notebook from Leo's hands. "Wait," she said before Leo could speak. Her voice shook in a way that brought a new pain to Leo's head. "Do you remember that story I told you? Of when I got lost in the woods as a kid? It wasn't long after your parents . . . "

"Yes, I remember. You saw a dead deer that scarred you for life. Tate, I want to leave—"

"I *didn't* see a deer. That's just what the people who found me guessed it was—they found one in the woods nearby after everything and assumed I saw that. But do you know what I really saw, Leo?" She flipped through the pages, many of them more damaged and falling apart than before.

Anger and guilt were slowly being replaced by apprehension. Something thrashed in the branches above them; more crows. A twig snapped between the trees to their backs. She turned in a slow circle, shining her flashlight into the woods. Its light only went so far before the night became impenetrable once again. "Tate—"

"I saw my own dead body." Tate stopped on a page and held it up for Leo to see. Scribbled notes illegible in the shadows. The flashlight moved to illuminate its pages. Leo could still barely make sense of the markings. "Only I was about ten years old then, and this looked like an older version of me. Like the age I am now. Eighteen."

"Calm down." Leo reached for her hand, but Tate snatched it away.

"No! I'm serious. It was my corpse. It was wearing a white shirt covered in blood and dirt, and I know it was me because the nose was crooked in the same place from when I broke it as a kid. Leaves and blood crusted up my hair, and there were maggots coming out of my eyes and mouth." Her voice broke. "I think I'm gonna die. Here, in Eston. I can never leave; I'm going to die here! I would die *anywhere else*. Just not here!" Tate's words spiraled, and she gestured to the book, eyes wild and feverish.

Leo took a shuddering breath. "Oh, Tate," she said softly. Her head ached where she'd been tense; now she was just scared. Tate's chest rose and fell visibly in her hysteria. "We need to go home." In slow motion, Leo reached forward and took the notebook from Tate's clutches. She was met with no resistance. Tate nearly collapsed into Leo's arms, body quaking with sobs. "We're okay. You're okay." Behind her back, Leo maneuvered the notebook so she could more closely see the two pages containing the frantic scribblings spelling out Tate's traumatic childhood vision. Sentence fragments and indecipherable strings of words. Whatever phrases she could make out confirmed all the gory details that Tate had said, and more disturbing ones beyond that. Leo felt tears sting the backs of her eyes. In one swift movement, she tore the pages out from the binding of the book. The sound of ripping paper was drowned out by Tate's crying. She stuffed the pages into her pocket.

Overhead, a chorus of crows squawked their dissent. Camouflaged by the night. A murder. Her hold on the terrified girl tightened.

Leo gently guided Tate out of the woods and through the Eston cemetery the way they'd come, refusing to spare a single glance back into whatever darkness dared to follow them.

AFTER

SHE KNEW SHE was being watched.

It was beyond the point of the hair standing up on the back of her neck, more than the goosebumps creeping along her arms, more than the auditory illusion of breathing in her ears. As she skated back to her aunt and uncle's house, a weight settled around her shoulders like a necklace of chains. Hugging her from behind like a phantasmagoric lover and threatening to pull down, down, down, off her skateboard and through the rain-soaked pavement, through the dirt and worms, the picked-clean bones, the earth's crust—and suffocating them both.

She focused on the sound of her old wheels against the sidewalk. A quiet, constant rush. The only comfort she could find in the town where she'd spent her life. It all looked different at night, though; the only light coming from sinister orange streetlamps that caught the leftover mists; alien movements on the other side of darkened windows; the familiar becoming strange.

Just get home, and it'll be fine. Maybe she could sleep when she got there. *But the pages.*

The last Leo had seen the spread of pages she had ripped out of Tate's notebook, she'd most likely left them buried in the pocket of her jeans, which had been discarded onto the floor of her bedroom for the better part of a week following that first fateful walk in the woods. She pictured herself skating up to her aunt and uncle's house, kicking the board to lean against the siding, and somehow ending up in her bedroom. Where had she stashed them again? The papers were crumpled, severely limiting whatever legibility that remained in Tate's scrawled handwriting. They were clear in her mind's eye, the softened texture almost tangible. Dizziness clouded her thoughts. She must have done something that alerted Sebago then, as the dog trotted into the room and nudged Leo's hands with her muzzle. A shaky breath escaped her lips as she gratefully scratched between Sebago's ears and sat on the floor so that the two were level.

"Thank you, Sebbie," she said, leaning against her bedframe. The pages, right, the pages. They'd found their way into her hands somehow. It was as if her eyes would not allow themselves to focus enough on the words in front of her so that she could read them fully. Perhaps this was a good thing. The few fragments she did catch from different parts of the page, standing out as if in a word search puzzle, were gruesome. But one final phrase held her attention captive. *Among the weeds, a corpse. Maggots where eyes used to be. My eyes. My rotting skin.* **I am not the only me**.

Sebago whined, and Leo flinched. A heavy paw prodded her leg a few times to emphasize her point. "Okay, okay, I know." She sucked in a deep breath and straightened her back, which was stiff, and offered more than one crack as she did so. It hadn't felt like she'd been sitting there for a long time—though the carpet had left sore imprints on her bare thighs, which also begged to differ.

Leo planted a kiss on the dog's head and then reached under the bed for a shoebox. It held a couple of knick-knacks, but only the kind that felt too raw to be on display in a room. An old picture of her parents as teenagers, a picture of Sebago as a little puppy, some bass picks (although she only used her fingers), a piece of sea glass, a Swiss Army knife. Winced and shook her head. Leo had folded the pages from Tate's notebook as neatly as she could before adding them to the small collection. Hoped she would be able to lock the contents of the shoebox back away into the recesses of her brain and move on. The box was pushed aside into its place under the bed.

A cold breeze on her face whipped Leo back to the present as she rode the skateboard through Eston's darkened streets. The pages would still be there in that box. Although the feeling of someone watching, of being followed at close range on her journey home, argued otherwise.

Leo realized too late that she was going a lot faster than she meant to. Her unbuttoned jacket billowed out behind her, and a few flyaway strands of hair tore free of her bun, streaming out in wakes. Fleeing from something that wasn't there. She skidded into her neighborhood and went through a turn that made her lose her balance on the board, wobbling on unsteady legs that didn't trust themselves. "*Shit!*"

She threw her weight and landed with a thud into the wet grass beside the sidewalk, but her ankle twisted with the movement. The now-abandoned skateboard careened ahead and was swallowed by the night.

Leo's groan, more out of frustration than pain, was the only sound to travel down the dreary road. The constant rush of the skateboard wheels was gone, leaving a thick silence. She looked all around her before she stood up, but, of course, there was nobody watching her. The street was barren in the night. Pavement in front of her and behind her, grass and trees on either side, a few streetlamps here and there casting the dark in an odd gold. Nobody following her.

Her twisted ankle was sore but could handle her weight so long as she tread carefully. She shuffled and brushed off as best she could. Dew soaked the back of Leo's shirt and pants, chafing her legs, but she didn't have time to care.

As she regained her footing on the sidewalk, a path she had walked down a million times and could map out every minute crack from memory, the last streetlamp up ahead caught a strange silhouette.

This was the final town-sanctioned light in the vicinity before the road officially branched off into dirt that eventually became Leo's driveway a little further down amongst the trees. Its too-orange glow glanced off the remnants of the day's rain, creating a halo around the tall bulb and a reflection on the damp tar below that stretched around in all directions. Against the dark, the streetlight looked more like a planet, a solitary orb of fire that would burn all it touched. Standing beneath the glow was a hulking figure on all fours. Its coarse fur stood up on end and caught the light, giving the illusion of a pelt made of fire. Being lit from above, most of its features remained in shadow, but it stood with an uneven posture that was somehow both muscular and skeletal, and its eyes reflected the same fiery blaze that traced its outline.

Leo remained frozen in place, locked in a staring contest with the creature. Her heart pounded in her ears. Didn't dare to blink. A fair distance separated them, but not enough—the thing stood between Leo and her home. And she'd lost her skateboard. She was cornered; it was hunting her.

A deep rumbling that could only be a growl carried through the air and sent tremors from the ground up Leo's legs and spine. The thing stepped fully into the lamplight then, baring fangs dripping with saliva. A wiry tail swished behind as it crouched, preparing to stalk in her direction. Much bigger than a wolf, with a rabid craze that hunched its shoulders and wrinkled its snout. Leo felt as though the air was knocked out of her. She had seen this monster in pictures before. In Tate's notebook, under the list of cryptids.

A black dog. The harbinger of death.

Leo took instinctive steps backward in time with the creature's slow hunting gait. Panic threatened to bubble in her stomach, up to her head, drown out every other thought. She bit it down. She needed to get Tate's pages.

The dog advanced. She could now clearly see the drool dripping from its fangs and curled lips, and despite having stepped closer to Leo and out of the streetlamp's grasp, its wide eyes still possessed that orange glow, devoid of pupils and unnaturally bright. Sinewy limbs almost creaked with each step it took on massive paws with unsheathed claws. Leo remained still. Though the tenseness in her muscles begged her to choose between fight or flight, she froze.

It was close enough now to disturb the loose strands of Leo's hair with its hot, rotten breath. She tried not to gag at the stench as flecks of spit splattered her face. The creature towered above her, the top of her head only just coming to its breastbone. It growled again, a low gargling noise channeled from deep within its body. The sound rumbled through Leo's own chest. She did not move.

Its wet nose leaned down and touched her shoulder, taking in a few quick sniffs. The dog smelled the skin of her neck, her tied-up hair. Taking inventory of the one it had condemned. Leo squinted against the huffs of rancid breath in her face. It snarled, louder than ever, teeth bared inches from her nose.

Then it turned and stalked beyond the treeline, away from the sidewalk and away from Leo. Its two glowing eyes were visible in the thick of the foliage for a split second, considering its eventual prey one last time; Orpheus glancing back at Eurydice, damnation in his eyes, and then it melted into the shadows completely.

Leo felt faint as all the blood drained from her face. The terror finally won out; she bolted down the road, nearly twisting the same ankle again, and arrived in her front yard in the span of just a few moments. The living room light shone through the windows, though she had no idea what time it was. Must have been late. But Leo barely slowed her stride up the few porch stairs and through the front door, slamming the screen and the heavy door shut behind her, making the whole house rattle.

"Jesus!" Uncle Mike exclaimed from his La-Z-Boy,

jolting up and spilling the remainder of his canned beer onto his lap.

Aunt Deb barreled into the living room, wielding a cooking pan above her head. Upon recognizing the hyperventilating girl leaning against the front door, she lowered the pan cautiously. "Leo. Tell me what's wrong." Her voice was stern, but she clasped the pan's handle with white knuckles.

"There's . . . I saw . . . " Leo panted, lungs aching with every heaved breath.

A scratching came from the other side of the door. Leo flung herself away, her back to the opposite wall. It had followed her. Her eyes were crazed and wide, her frame tensed like a cornered animal. She got ready to run.

"It's just Sebago, honey," Aunt Deb said, walking over to let the dog inside with a puzzled look at Leo.

"Oh, Sebbie." Leo collapsed to her knees as her dog bounded through the door and licked her face gleefully. *Can't have you going outside right now, buddy. You're staying with me.* Relief made the dizziness return, and she leaned her forehead on Sebago's soft shoulder. Wanted to melt into the warm, familiar texture.

"Leonora, I need you to tell me what's going on. Right now." Aunt Deb was now visibly shaken, staring at her from across the room. She made no attempt at approaching her niece.

Leo couldn't say it. *Oh, no big deal, just ran into a spectral demon dog outside that's an ancient omen for an oncoming death. Which proves the validity of at least some of Tate's theories from that stupid notebook. All is good and dandy.* She glanced up at her aunt, scrambling for an excuse. "I'm—I feel sick," Leo stuttered, still breathing heavily.

Aunt Deb's posture relaxed a little. "Yeah, I can tell," she said. "You could blend in with a blizzard, you're so pale. Why don't you go to bed, then, eh? Only nine or so, but you could use the sleep, dear." Leo felt as though she were ripped out of time and thrown back into the wrong place. Sebbie licked her cheek.

Leo stood in a daze, operating on autopilot. "Okay," she said. Mike and Deb's apprehensive stares followed her out of the living room, but neither said another word. Sebago trotted at her heels.

Her bedroom door closed with a quiet click. Leo sunk to the floor and hugged her knees while Sebago assumed her position, laying down with her chin by Leo's toes. And Leo cried.

Full dark, no stars. Wheezes and gasps made her ribs rattle and heave. The black dog—a portent of death. The mere presence of the apparition was a death sentence. Leo might as well be a walking corpse; she doubted she'd see the sun rise the next day.

The dissonance between Leo's body and her thoughts grew, and she was untethered. She felt the presence of her Swiss Army knife tucked away in the shoebox with a phantom stinging in her wrists, which might as well have been miles away. Maybe it would be better to finish the job before whatever hells she and Tate had evoked that summer came back to haunt her. She could die on her own terms and be safe. Stifle her doubt until it suffocated. Far, far away from the small town she thought she knew inside and out, but which possessed an anathema array of secrets just beyond her house's doorframe. And also, possibly, within it. A stillness settled about the bedroom like the disquiet of a graveyard.

Strange, awful tranquility. The only light in the room came from the icy blue hue of a nightlight plugged into the wall. The certainty of death was like an old friend. Everyone dies, Ava Bates had died and taken Kenneth with her, and Leo Bates would follow them off stage into the void that lingered beyond the curtain and was never meant to be seen. She hovered outside of herself and thought that death may not be so very different from this. The dissonance, the familiar dissociation. It would be a comforting thing to surrender. Accept damnation's kiss to her open veins.

The calm brought with it an opportunity for fear to trickle in. Leo watched herself across the room lower her head to the floor, clench her arms around her body tighter and groan. It wasn't the fear of dying but fear on another's behalf. Tate Mulder. Calling out to her on the other side of the abyss once again.

The black dog. Had Tate seen it, too, before she disappeared? Nothing could soothe the horror as she pictured it. Primal fear had rooted Leo to the pavement, locked in a staring contest with a creature she had only learned about in old legends retold by Tate a couple of months before, had not thought it existed, and yet there it was, daring her to doubt it and instilling an animalistic terror that caught her skeleton in an electric current and paralyzed her. She didn't want to think about Tate ever feeling that way. Had it appeared to her, all dripping yellow fangs and hulking anatomy and glowing eyes, so she knew she would die before it happened—

A violent, physical rejection of the thought made Leo nauseous. No, Tate wouldn't have seen it because she had to be alive. *Had* to be. Tate Mulder was the only person in Eston, the only person on earth that would know what to do now. Ironically, she was the only person Leo knew that had the knowledge of the unexplained—the obsession with it—to solve her own disappearance. And that's why Leo had to find her.

Tonight.

Hands working of their own volition reached beneath the bed. Leo rolled over sluggishly on the carpet and gazed into the crawlspace. Fingers brushed the old shoebox before her eyes adjusted enough to see it. There was a ringing in her ears that wouldn't cease. She pulled the box out and opened it.

Tate's pages were still there, folded with care and pinned beneath Leo's knife. Her fingers caressed the sheathed blade. She squeezed her eyes shut until she saw stars.

Leo released a breath she forgot she had been holding and cracked her knuckles, grounding her thoughts back to her body. She reached into the box quickly and pushed the knife aside as if the metal burned her skin. She took the papers and pressed them close to her chest, lying with her back flat on the carpeted floor. Sebago offered one soft whine, swishing her tail as she crawled forward to rest her chin on Leo's thigh. "We're okay," Leo exhaled, gripping the dog's collar loosely as she stared at the ceiling. She had honestly forgotten she was there.

BEFORE

TATE BARELY SAID a word as they drafted back to the car. They had parked a long ways out from the woods, but they were going at a much faster pace now than when they had arrived at the cemetery earlier that evening. And plus, now they were empty-handed—except for a flashlight and Tate's notebook.

Out from under the cover of the leafless trees, the earth held its breath with the return of the girls. The crows lost interest, and the leaves were silent save for their footsteps. It was still early in the night—couldn't be much past eight— but the stars glowered down like holes in a black sheet, piercings that smuggled enough meager white light to guide their way.

It went without saying that Leo would have to drive. With one hand still gently resting on the small of Tate's back, she opened the passenger's side door and coaxed her inside. She moved to obstruct Tate's view of the woods whenever her gaze started wandering in the direction of that void. Had to avert her own stare more than once.

A shaky huff escaped Tate as she sat down in her car. Leo shut the door and hurried to get in the driver's seat, and the old Nissan pulled away without comment.

There was nothing she could say. So when they finally turned onto the main road, off of the cemetery grounds, Leo said the only words she could think of. "Love you, Tate."

Tate sniffled. "I love you." She had her knees pulled up

to her chest and hugged them tightly. Leo didn't bother telling her to wear her seatbelt. The tattered notebook was shoved onto the floor under the passenger seat, jostling along the journey.

Before either of them realized it, Leo shifted the car into park, and they sat in Tate's driveway. The windows were dark, and all was still on the inside. Didn't seem like her mother, Marion, was home. Tate grasped Leo's wrist before she could release the gearshift, and Leo flinched. "I don't want to be alone," she said. If she was honest, Leo didn't either. They went inside the empty house, hand in white-knuckled hand.

It was a dreamy climb up the carpeted stairs to Tate's bedroom, and every shadow leered at them from the walls. They kept the lights off lest they be seen—by what, neither could articulate. Leo held on to the back of Tate's shirt like a lifeline. Muffled steps and ringing ears underlined the bending of reality. How could they return to normalcy after what they'd seen in those woods? They had almost been crushed by that door, and yet only now it seemed Leo's chest was ready to implode. The stairs marked the meeting place of one reality and another, the before and the after, and in reaching the top, Leo and Tate were confronted with the strange familiarity of something as mundane as a young adult girl's childhood bedroom.

The room was all blues and blacks like a bruise. To turn on the lights would be to cut their shapes out of the dark, leaving them overexposed and naked. Inverted shadow-puppets. Leo was perfectly content letting her eyes adjust to the only source of halfhearted light coming from the window over Tate's queen-sized bed.

Tate threw her thick notebook somewhere into the abyss, and it vanished. Probably onto a pile of clothes or among the extra pillows that she had a habit of hoarding. Leo didn't need to see her bedroom to visualize these landmarks. With a creak, Tate crawled onto the mattress. Leo watched in the darkness and then tried her best to ground herself and follow her lead. They lay side by side on the unmade bed in silence for what seemed like a long time, not touching. The act of breathing felt like an exaggerated movement that she was too aware of. She felt herself start to slip away, staring at the ceiling.

Then, to Leo's amazement, Tate began to laugh. A real, convulsing laugh that left her breathless and summoned Leo back to this moment in the bedroom. The sound bounced off the walls like they were in an echo chamber. Tate was beautiful when she laughed. Absurd, intoxicating. It was impossible not to return a grin in the contagious delirium, and Leo did so through gritted teeth and pressed the heels of her hands hard into her eyes until she saw dizzying shapes and colors. Tate's laughter rattled Leo's chest as the girl rolled over and buried her face in her shoulder.

"How's . . . how's that . . . for proof, huh?" Tate said in between heaves of breath that mimicked her sobs from not an hour before. Tears dampened Leo's shirt as Tate wrapped an arm tight around her waist and tangled their legs together.

"I don't feel good," Leo said. The feeling of Tate's smooth skin against her own made the room spin.

"I don't see how you would." Tate caught her breath with a long exhale and then squirmed up to brush her lips on Leo's collarbone where the neckline of her shirt had been pulled askew. "You believe me now, right? That there's something weird about this town? And the woods! Something . . . *unexplainable!*" She was nearly giddy. "That door, dude. It's something big. Shit, I wish we hadn't broken it."

Leo made a sound from deep in her throat and cradled both arms around Tate, kissing the crown of her forehead lightly. The gesture was subconscious and surprised Leo herself. "I don't feel good," she repeated in a muffled, lowered voice. The childlike claim seemed to be the only thing she could say. The image of Tate staring unblinking into the void behind the stone door, no irises, no expression, flashed through her mind like a specter. Felt like a knife thrust between her eyes. She wanted to melt into their embrace, the only safe sensation she had felt in a long time.

A silence fell over them again. Silvery streaks streamed through the blinds in the window and left faded stripes over their bodies. Precise, geometric vectors met with organic and imperfect things. Broken by the slope of Tate's hip, the softness of the exposed fraction of her stomach, the bend at Leo's knee, and draped over their faces like half-formed masks. Tate moved her hand up and traced the outline of Leo's jaw, fingertips caressing the soft angle there that was made extreme by the fractured light. Goosebumps rose at the touch as Leo watched the thin shadows of the blinds receding off Tate with each movement. The displaced shadows were followed by others which bent and curved to fit the mold of her body. Warm-toned eyes reflected the gashes of moonlight and almost forgot their natural vibrant hue. One particular vector of shadow lay perfectly in line with Tate's half-parted lips, giving the appearance of an eerie flat smile stretching across the width of her face. Heart pounding, hands trembling, Leo moved forward and broke the shadow with her own mouth.

The events of the night forgotten, or at least suppressed enough, Leo was insane with the need to be closer to Tate. Needed to reach inside her ribcage and make a home there in the all-encompassing warmth. She deepened the kiss, and her hand wandered off its own volition up the back of Tate's shirt to unhook her bra in one skillful motion, which made Leo seem a lot more well-versed in this type of thing than she actually was. Tate moaned into Leo's mouth and gently grazed her teeth off her lower lip. All points of contact were electrified and hypersensitive. Only partly aware of her actions, Leo pressed closer and closer until she was straddling Tate's hips, pinning the now-shirtless girl down to the bed with most of her weight.

"I'll make you feel better." There was a grin in Tate's voice as she sucked hard at a point on Leo's neck. She gasped, lowering her head down into the crook of Tate's shoulder. Heat crept up her spine, and soon Leo was shirtless as well. Dizzy with skin-on-skin contact, hot to the touch, a full-body blush sneaking over Leo's pale chest as it always did. She kissed her neck, felt the racing pulse there with the delicate skin of her lips. Tate arched her back, and Leo moved down her body, pressing her mouth first between her breasts, trailing down to her naval. A feverish unbuttoning of skinny jeans and unbound hair falling around Tate's hips in a curtain. And she went lower, holding Tate's thighs close to either side of her head, muffling out the world. They were doomed, and damned. Leo was rapture incarnate and ached to hold her as tightly, as closely, as possible—as if to pull Tate back from that door in the woods, from her morbid fascination, and drink in every aspect of her being for herself.

Neither girl regarded the notebook on the floor or the grotesque pages it had fallen open to.

Delicious coziness cushioned Leo's bare back as Tate cuddled up against her under the covers. Breath stirred the hair at the back of her neck. She'd lost an elastic at some point, so her fiery tresses hung freely. Tate brushed a stray strand out of Leo's face from behind and kissed the top of her head.

Night hung over them like a veil. But, despite her exhaustion, Leo would not fall asleep.

"Tate?"

One of her long fingers traced a circular pattern on Leo's stomach, leaving tired butterflies in its wake. "Hmm?" Tate said dreamily.

A presence in the room felt like dead weight on her lungs. Open pages on the floor, hidden by shadows but real all the same. "I want you to get rid of that notebook."

Without needing to turn, she could picture the dismay on Tate's face. She went still behind her, fingers freezing on Leo's hip. "What?"

"You heard me."

A hand gently bore down on Leo's shoulder so that she now rested on her back and could look Tate in the eyes. She was startled by their severity. "That's *months'* worth of research, Leo . . . "

"I know. But it's just—it's too much. I don't think it's healthy for you." *Or me.*

"'Cause of the door? Look, I know that was dangerous, it could have fallen on us, but I didn't know it would be that fragile. I'd never gotten that close before. I'm gonna have to research some more." Leo just stared at her, and Tate blinked. Then her eyes suddenly widened with understanding. "Oh," she said. "This is because of those pages with your parents." She quieted her voice. "I'm sorry you saw that."

Leo's voice cracked. "Why do you have that stuff in there?" Images of Ava and Kenneth sitting under a tree, far too pale, far too limp. A scene that Leo had imagined plenty of times, but never actually seen in such blunt, merciless clarity.

She brushed Leo's jawline with a feather-light touch. "Because I think there's more to every story. Even the ones we think we have all the answers to." Her tone was quiet, almost pleading. "Sometimes there's something off. At the crux of the story, something that doesn't make sense, regardless of all the hard evidence you can get. And then it's up to you to find that missing key. That notebook," she gestured somewhere into the darkness away from the bed, "that's full of potential keys. Not just for unlocking the mystery of your parents. But to the dead body—*my* dead body—that I found in the woods years ago. To that door we went to today behind the cemetery. To *all* of Eston. All the kids who get lost in the woods here every year. Unexplained phenomena like that. Conspiracies and cryptids. Could maybe even unlock the whole world and the rest of its urban legends."

Leo's scowl slowly etched itself between her eyebrows, although her voice remained soft. "Why do *you* have to be the one to find the keys?"

"I don't. I think you do."

She almost flinched. Tate suddenly got up and searched for the book in the dark, still naked. The way she padded about the room, only half-covering her breasts, would have brought the sweetest of smiles to Leo's face if she wasn't so startled by what she'd said. Tate dropped the book on the bed with a thud. Grabbed a blanket and wrapped it around her shivering body. Leo sat up after a moment with Tate's heavier blanket and tried not to touch the damaged bundle of papers by her feet. She huddled in close until Tate eventually opened up and wrapped both their blankets around their shoulders together, bare skin next to skin. The infatuation was enough to forget the horrors—if only for a moment.

The pages made a satisfying crinkling sound as Tate leafed through them. "It's weird," she said. "I feel like a lot of things come back around to you and your family. Did you know, in the general area where your parents died— just about exactly on the town line and far enough away from the main road that nobody out for a walk could see them—and following that line around Eston, there's been seven cases of either death or missing people? Approximately one per year since they died. And there's some cases from before them, too. I don't remember hearing anything about this stuff in the news. But the clippings are here. *All* near the town line."

Tate must have been carefully avoiding the spread with Leo's parents because she didn't see it through all her flipping. What she did see was a familiar stretch of forest appearing in the black and gray newspaper articles more than once. Though it was likely only familiar in the way that all forests are familiar, she reminded herself.

The headlines were unsettling nonetheless. Missing children, found children, elderly dementia patients wandering off, perfectly healthy young adults suffering mental breakdowns, corpses long decomposed—all taking place in the Eston woods, often near the very edge of town. There were other things, too. From books more so than newspapers. Strange sightings not only contained to their tiny hometown but spread throughout Maine. A three-eyed deer, one article said. An apish humanoid form. A bipedal, antlered creature. A hellhound, a black dog.

Of course, Leo had seen many of these clippings and notes the first time she'd glanced through Tate's notebook while on their way to the woods behind the graveyard. However, now these things instilled a tenseness in the way she gripped Tate's inner arm, which wasn't there before and which neither girl acknowledged.

Leo found herself watching Tate's long fingers move rather than the pictures they were flipping through. Her throat tightened, and she thought she might be sick. She rubbed at one of her eyes. Needed to say it. "If you wanted to know about my parents, you could have just asked me." Not an ounce of either malice or self-pity was in her tone; Leo felt like the last lonely snowflakes piling onto the banks from the blizzard that came before. Post-devastation gentleness that does nothing to ease the pains already wrought. Never mind that had Tate actually inquired about the loss of her parents at any point before, Leo would never have told Tate exactly what she'd wanted to find out.

Tate said nothing for a moment and licked her lips. The lower lip was a little swollen where Leo had bitten down too hard. "I'm sorry. You're right. I just wanted to know . . . " She trailed off, as if ready to say more, and then repeated with more conviction: "I wanted to *know*. And you're hard enough to read as it is. I couldn't risk scaring you away. I need you."

"You don't scare me, Tate Mulder," Leo spoke with a smirk that didn't reach her eyes.

Tate huffed with a sad sort of amusement. "Maybe I should."

Leo paused, took a breath to ask Tate what she meant, when her bedroom door burst open. Tate screamed, and Leo tightened her grasp on Tate's arm, trying to shield her under the blanket. A tall, backlit figure reached a slender limb out for the light switch and blinded them with an artificial yellow-whiteness.

Marion Mulder stared at them from the doorframe to her daughter's bedroom. "*Leo!*" she exhaled with enough relief to soften her frightening entrance. At least a little bit. She still wore her greenish scrubs from the night shift at the hospital. "You girls know how late it is? Your aunt called me all panicked, has no idea where you are!" Quickly Marion seemed to register the two girls huddled together under one blanket, suspiciously close and suspiciously covered. They stared back at her with mortified eyes. She blinked, then looked away. "Oh, sorry. Um." Tate's mother shuffled, and Leo resisted the urge to curl up and hide away. "You know you're always welcome here, sweetie. But out of respect for Deb, I need to let her know where you are. And Tate, you know Deb's new rule. You two can't be sneaking around like this."

Tate started again. "Mama—"

"Take a moment to get dressed, and I'll drive you home, Leo." Marion lingered with her hand on the doorknob. She made uncomfortable eye contact with her daughter, who was like her in so many ways. "I'm sorry, honey." And with that, she left.

They retrieved their clothes from the floor without a word. Tate shut the notebook and kicked it under her bed unceremoniously. Leo watched her motions with a blush and then caught her own eye in a mirror, overly aware of the already-darkening spattering of hickeys on her neck. The reflection was unfamiliar.

The drive back to her aunt and uncle's house was nauseating and tense. Leo had stared as Tate's figure receded into the distance of the rearview, standing on the porch under the orange light of the motion sensor. She was still standing there when the light turned off, and Marion pulled out of the driveway.

Cheeks flushed, Leo kept her head angled toward the window so as not to catch Marion's undoubtedly horrified expression. So it startled her when the woman spoke with such a degree of kindness. "I don't know if this is the right thing to do," Marion admitted. Neither looked at the other. A pause as the car rumbled over a small pothole. "My daughter cares about you a lot. I hate to hurt her like this. But, y'know, your aunt's much older than I am, and she'll probably skin me alive for turning a blind eye to you two spending the night together after what happened a few weeks ago."

The bruises on Leo's knuckles had faded since the encounter with the boy. A flare of anger stung the places in her hands that had been all shades of purple, green, and red. Tate had kissed them so gently.

"I don't want you to get in trouble, either, Leo. For the record, I don't think it's fair. But it wouldn't be smart of me to go against your aunt's wishes when she's so passionate about them. God knows what she must think of Tate and I . . . " Her tone wavered for a moment, and then her face hardened along with her resolve. "*Fuck* her opinion, honestly. It's just that I can't have her harassing us—not that she is right now, she has a right to be concerned for her niece—but I'm not even sure how she got my phone number. She called me six times tonight to see if I knew where you were. She was *pissed*. I just want what's best for Tate."

Leo hesitated, fixating on her healed-back-to-pale knuckles. She took a shaky breath. "Me, too," she said in a small voice.

Marion glanced at her out of the corner of her eye. They turned into Leo's driveway and parked, and before she could say anything, Marion cautiously took Leo's phone out of her hands and added herself as a contact. "Take care of yourself, honey," she said, and returned the phone. Leo's heart hurt.

Heedless of the warnings Leo gave, Marion insisted on walking her up to the house. Aunt Deb's rage was predictable. Leo did her best to absorb most of the initial outburst and give Marion a chance to get away, but not before Deb had exclaimed that her daughter was "*never* allowed to take Leo away like this again!" Tate's mother listened to the storm with narrowed eyes and with her full lips pressed into an inflexible line.

Despite Marion's previously stated sympathies, the two were kept apart for the following few weeks of the summer. Leo was largely confined to the house and the yard. A ticking time bomb, she knew. Ripped some dead grass out from the ground where she sat. Thirst for Tate's presence made her anxious and temperamental, like a starving vampire. She hoped that Tate wouldn't undergo any more excursions to the site beyond the cemetery without her, but somehow knew that the hope was futile. Hoped that she wouldn't get herself into more trouble. Wondered what more trouble would mean for her research. Speculation got her heart racing. What macabre revelations would Tate uncover without Leo? Where else could these fascinations take her? Tate had said that a lot of Eston's mysteries came back around to Leo and her family, but Leo rather thought the opposite. A younger Tate had gotten lost in the woods and was terrified, sure; that happens to a lot of kids. But that vision she had. Why Tate, of all people?

Perhaps it was time for Leo to do some research of her own.

AFTER

A FUNNY THING happens after prolonged dissociation. You start to lose your body. Lying completely motionless on the floor, staring at the ceiling for such a time that you lose sensation of the carpet beneath you. Aren't seeing the popcorn ceiling hovering above. Can't hear the rhythmic breathing of the dog beside you, let alone your own breathing. Leo had no outline; her outer limits extended to the floor, to Sebbie, her bed, the rest of the house. She was not just Leo but a gathering of objects, pieces of a consciousness detached. Whether she was floating or falling, she could not tell.

Some people call this meditation, she supposed. Or maybe hypnosis. The feeling reminded her of playing bass. Being able to separate her mind from her body and let her fingers strum away. It was peaceful, almost. The difference was that when she played bass, she could snap herself out of it. Right now, Leo felt stuck. She was there, in her bedroom with Sebbie half-asleep at her side—but she wasn't. Perhaps her mother had felt this way sometimes.

She was held in place by a force both within her and without. Her physical body was in a space that pinned her to the floor and felt her anxiety at a distance, while another allowed her mind to drift sluggishly up and out of the cage of her skull. Tate herself could have been lying beside her, and Leo would've been none the wiser. Wraithlike while they floated. Like they were in the woods again. Leaves formed a soft bed beneath them, some kind of wildflower

111

(or maybe a weed) caught in Tate's tight curls, the same plant tucked behind Leo's ear, a delicate display, and then more would grow around them, sprouting from the leaves as they stared into each other's eyes, wrapping stems around their wrists, ankles, shoulders, necks, in decadent decay, beginning to obscure their eyesight now, sinking into the mud, the weeds would grow into their ears, noses, mouths, bore holes in their throats and turn black as they let the forest reclaim their bodies.

The girl and dog rested there for mere moments that felt like an eternity. Leo started by flexing her fingers, wiggling her toes, clenching fists. Heard the crinkle of the notebook pages as she touched them with one hand. An attempt to will herself out of that state of suspended animation by reminding her consciousness that it was, in fact, connected to a body—for the time being. Suddenly her bedroom door opened with a creak, which would have normally made her jump had she been more present, and Sebago tensed and flattened her ears at whoever peered inside.

Aunt Deb leaned around the ajar door and seemed startled to find her niece on the floor. She flicked the light switch, and the lamp on Leo's bedside table left aching remnants of light on the insides of her eyelids. "What are you doing?" Deb questioned, still not fully stepping into the room.

Leo pushed herself up with an immense effort and rubbed her eyes with one hand. She placed Tate's pages behind her back with the other. "Nothing. Sitting with Sebbie." Her words were drowsy and slow.

"You're acting weird." The unnatural yellow light cast harsh contours on Deb's face that didn't do much to complement it. Leo squinted. There was a pause, and then her aunt tiptoed into the bedroom and leaned on the door to shut it with a gentle latch behind her back. Leo's skin prickled, still coming out of her reverie. Deb took a breath and wouldn't look her niece in the eye. She was wearing an old crewneck sweatshirt and pajama pants, hair tied back behind her neck, and shadows under her eyes. Leo had never realized how tired her aunt looked, how little rest she had gotten these past three days. It made Leo irrationally irritated, as if Aunt Deb had a right to be in pain over Tate. Finally, she spoke. "Everyone grieves differently, Leo, but it's not healthy for you to obsess over that girl like this. Especially if . . . if you were involved."

Leo's jaw dropped, sobered. The words were plain, not angry nor sad. "I didn't do anything."

Deb exhaled slowly. "You were the last one to see her, sweetheart. If you didn't do anything, what happened?"

It was dark, foggy in the woods and her mind alike. Her lips parted to speak, ready as if the answer were obvious, but no words came to the surface. Leo realized she had no idea exactly what had happened the last time she was with Tate. Her memory was blank, like it was wiped clean by some external force. She'd been with her . . . somewhere . . . and then she was back in her bedroom, alone. The gaps in her memory scared her more than anything else she'd seen in Tate's notebook or in the woods beyond the Eston cemetery.

"It's my job to keep you safe, no matter what," Deb continued, heedless of Leo's shock. "Your mother trusted me to do that. Even with all the times we fought. You know, a few months before she, er . . . well, she said that if anything were to happen to her that I should take you in. I was confused. I wanted to say no. Barely knew you, anyway. Why should I take care of my kid sister's little troublemaker? But there was something in the way she'd asked me. We hadn't talked in over a year, see. She just showed up here one day. Mike and I had just moved in. I heard a knock at the door. A real slow one.

"Ava was different from the last time I'd seen her. She was terrified. Of what, I never found out. Don't think I want to know, to this day." Aunt Deb tucked a strand of wiry brown hair behind her ear and folded her arms. "But

I invited her in. Er, she *asked* if she could come in. So I got Mike to put some coffee on, and we talked for a bit. Probably the most honest talk we ever had."

Leo swallowed with a throat of broken glass. "Why are you telling me this?" Sebago gazed back and forth between them, sensing the tension.

Her aunt glowered down at her and opened her mouth for a retort and then, with a strain, smoothed her expression back over. "You're just like her, y'know. She told me she'd been having bad dreams. That used to happen a lot when we were kids. I would wake up in the middle of the night to her screaming on the other side of the wall. Thought she grew out of it, but I guess not. She told me that she was afraid for you. *For* you. And she wanted me to take care of you if anything went wrong with her and Kenneth. Those were her words, not mine: if anything went wrong. I was scared myself at this point. She got all mad that I was hesitating, but I finally agreed. Then she just left."

The height difference between herself sitting on the floor and Deb standing was making Leo uneasy. She rose to her feet so that their eyes were level.

Aunt Deb shuffled her weight. "My point is, Leo, you and your mom both have—had—this habit. You're distant, but you let things get to you. Close everyone out but get obsessed and paranoid when you're left alone for too long. It drove your mum off the edge, and she dragged your dad down with her. She knew you were like her. I'm not going to let the same thing happen to you."

Leo blanched. There was a long silence before she could gather any words to form a response. "This is different. Something bad happened to Tate. It's something only she and I would understand." Reckless honesty made her voice steady, her gaze unfaltering. "I don't remember what happened three nights ago, the last time I saw her. I really don't, and I didn't realize that until now, and that terrifies the shit out of me. You coming in here, you talking about my mom—it made me think of something." The doorway in the woods, its multiple collapses, Tate's vision of her own dead body, the Talbot twins' deaths, her mother's suicide. "I think I know what to do. I'm going to get her back."

Losing her patience, Deb picked at the fraying threads in the elbow of her sweater. "Leo, if you were involved in her disappearance, it's understandable. Things like this can be hereditary. It wasn't your fault—I can get you the help your mother never got. And you'll be okay."

"No. It's not understandable. It's *unexplainable*." Without thinking, part of her still detached, Leo walked over to her window. The one she and Tate had watched receive a splattering of crow feathers and blood that one summer day. The murder of crows. Tucked Tate's scribblings into her back pocket. She lifted the window open. Sebago followed.

Aunt Deb stepped closer. "Hey, hey, what are you—"

"Just this once, Deb, I need you to trust me. Please." Leo swung a leg through the opening, straddling the windowsill. Her sneaker brushed the tallest of the weeds creeping up the side of the house a couple of feet below.

A hand fastened around Leo's forearm like a vise, acrylic nails digging into her skin. Sebago growled. Leo stared into her aunt's eyes and felt heat rise to her cheeks. "This is different," she repeated. A softer voice than she had ever used in an argument with her aunt. Almost childlike in its sincerity. "Tate is *alive*."

Moments passed. Aunt Deb released her grip. "The woods," she said. "You're going there, aren't you?"

She ducked through the window and jumped to the ground before Deb could stop her. Her feet hit the damp ground with a thud, and a scrambling of claws on the windowsill ended in Sebago clumsily tumbling out after her. Aunt Deb shouted something from inside, her calm demeanor finally snapped. Sebbie looked up at Leo and waited for a command with a loyalty that pained her. No use trying to get her back in the house. "Come on," Leo said, and the dog ran alongside her to the front yard.

Pounding footsteps and muffled obscenities told her that Aunt Deb was going to meet them out front whether they liked it or not. How would she get to the cemetery fast enough with no skateboard? The encounter with the black dog had left Leo unable to go find it in the underbrush after she'd bailed during her frantic ride home. It was lost somewhere up the street.

Sebago rounded the corner of the house before Leo did and activated the motion-detecting light. Ghastly yellow reflected off the wet grass, caught the moths and bugs swarming the bulb. More shouts from the interior, this time joined by Uncle Mike's guttural and seldom-used yell. She couldn't make out what he was saying, but his animosity seemed targeted at Aunt Deb rather than Leo.

The sudden light made an object sitting in the dirt driveway visible. Her skateboard. Waiting as patiently as ever. Sebbie circled it and barked as if urging Leo onward.

After a stunned second, she sprinted forward and picked up the board without slowing down. Sebago ran diligently by her side, and they hit the neighborhood's pavement just as Aunt Deb, now a distant silhouette, opened the front door. She made no further effort to pursue them, and the motion-detecting light turned off.

Leo turned away. She hopped onto her skateboard, the familiar rumble of the wheels sending a chill up her shaky legs. Sebago panted by her hip and easily kept up the pace, claws clicking against the tar with each stride.

"To whatever horrors may find us," Leo said breathlessly, as Tate might have in that moment. They hurtled into the dark. Back under the orange streetlamp. No sign of the black dog. Back to the main road. The town center. The cemetery, the woods. She had the sense of boundaries being crossed, like a hole cut in a chain link fence with this one sliver of actionable information, the first idea she'd allowed to surface in these last three days.

The ripped pages of Tate's notebook stung in her pocket. All points led to the woods. That doorway they'd found in the summer.

Tate would be there.

THE REST OF the summer was tedious and blistering, and
it bled into the start of Leo's senior year of high
school. Though it was not without some bitter
amusement that Leo had anticipated the start of school.
Aunt Deb's embargo on her relationship had its
limitations, the most important of which being that she
could not prevent her from seeing Tate during school
hours. Never mind that Tate had been absent the first day
of class. Leo took it as a sign to keep up the persistence. In
the meantime, that fourth day of September, Leo would
need to busy herself with more accessible matters.

It was so easy to picture Tate sitting in the Eston Public
Library or wandering through the stacks alone like a ghost.
Checking out everything from encyclopedias of
cryptozoology to accounts of local history to textbooks on
psychology. And then there was more, up the rickety set of
rusty metal stairs that began behind an eternally-closed
door in the lobby. She could imagine the dust that floated
upward, disturbed at Tate's presence from the weeks
before, as the same particles drifted about in time with
Leo's movements now. The upstairs of the library was
considerably darker than the ground floor and
unfrequented by most, with the exception of the odd
neighborhood scholar. One needed a key from the front
desk to get up here. Some more valuable archival pieces
were said to lay hidden in the stacks, but Leo couldn't
imagine anything of modern merit tucked away in such

solitude. Tate was the upstairs library's most frequent
visitor, and the sparse group of employees recognized her
well enough to set aside the key for her whenever she was
spotted wandering the main floor.

The rows of bare lightbulbs that dangled above each
aisle did little more than expose the copious amounts of
dust and cobwebs that lingered on the highest of the old
metal shelves. The only other time Leo had been up here
at all was to accompany Tate earlier in the summer. When
she had been more bemused than troubled by her interests.
Now, she was alone; the wrinkled clerk named Mrs. Annie,
who had been working there since the beginning of time,
it seemed, had asked where her "little friend" was. Leo just
smiled tightly and said that Tate was busy, so she had sent
her along to pick up a volume or two. She supposed it
wasn't too far from the truth.

The sea of books in the upstairs library stacks stretched
farther than Leo could make out. There were no windows
and little ventilation. Sweat dripped down Leo's spine after
just moments of walking around. She would need to make
this quick.

Leo could only guess how long Tate had been at it.
Months, at least; her research had begun far before the two
of them ever grew close. The upper-level aisles felt
haphazard and nonsensical, with not much organization
that she could identify. Regardless, Tate had seemed to
know the place well when she brought Leo. She tried to
retrace the path that the two of them had taken before, but
all the weathered cloth- and leather-bound books blended
into one indistinguishable volume, a thick layer of dust
locking its manifold secrets inside. She turned a corner and
sneezed.

At last, sweat plastering the escaped strands of hair
from her low knot to her temples, Leo came upon a pair of
empty shelves near the back of the space. Though they
weren't entirely empty, per se. Whereas the rest of the
aisles were filled to the brim with books, double-parked in

some places, these two shelves contained a small selection of curated pieces—books, newspapers, a portfolio of some kind, a few VHS tapes, and DVDs. This is where Tate kept the rest of her research which she could not carry in her notebook.

Untying the flannel around her waist, Leo laid it flat on the wooden floor and sat cross-legged on top of it in front of the shelves. She rubbed at her eyes, itchy with dust, and started looking through the collection, ignoring the unease which prickled the hair on the back of her neck. And she got to work.

Her reasoning was straightforward. If Tate could dig up those things about her parents, about *her,* then Leo should be able to do the same in return. It's not that Tate had ever lied—she hoped—but there were more things she wasn't sharing beyond her interest in Leo's family history. Things about Tate herself, with any luck. Surely Tate would have collected anything that mentioned either of their lineages here, any evidence of past traumas. For control, so that she would know all the old wounds that might be opened down the line. Well, for the first time, Leo would be keeping all the puzzle pieces that she could find here for herself.

Although finding missing puzzle pieces would imply that they could get something more out of this. Out of all this drive to *know* and to *question,* to see it all fit together in some bigger picture at the end. Where Tate looked into the abyss and saw potential, the comfort of certainty—Leo looked and saw a pair of eyes staring back at them. And the eyes were angry.

Leo exhaled through her teeth. Might as well start from the beginning. She picked up the first thing on Tate's shelves, a small box collecting three VHS tapes. The box was unlabeled, but the first of the tapes had a long white sticker along its spine, with scrawled black handwriting that looked all too familiar. *CRYPT COLLAPSE*, Tate had written. *1995*. The other tapes had no such stickers and remained stubbornly anonymous. She put them back in their imprints of dust on the shelf.

One of the books leaning up against the box of tapes was thinner and taller than the rest. A yearbook: Eston Public High, class of 1995. It was the year her parents had graduated. Leo hesitated but had to leaf through the faded pages, and there they were. Kenneth White, lingering in the back of a few candids, and Ava Bates, mid-laugh with a few other girls. Leo would be the same age as them in these pictures. She turned the page, and there was one snapshot of them together, along with two other kids, a boy and a girl who looked very much alike. These were the Talbot twins, Bryce and Mackenzie; their defined jawlines and wispy hair were mirrors not only of themselves but also Jonathan, the boy Leo had punched earlier in the summer, their nephew. Leo chewed her lip.

The photo must've been taken when Ava, Kenneth, Bryce, and Mackenzie were in their band and played in the high school talent show. Darkness Visible, the outfit was called. They'd won, of course—to the dismay of the faculty who had originally prohibited their particular brand of punk rock vulgarity and angst to play at the show. Kenneth had told the story with pride more than once.

A smile crept at the edges of Leo's mouth. It was an action shot, with Kenneth on drums and Ava playing what would later become her daughter's bass guitar. Ava was looking over her shoulder at the boy so that her face was mostly obscured, but the wild red hair was unmistakable and not unlike Leo's. She couldn't resist taking a picture of the photo with her phone.

At the same time as the click of her phone's camera, a sharp sound erupted from the stacks behind her, like a book falling. Leo whipped to face the direction it had come from, but at least two aisles separated her from the noise. Towers of archived materials without the slightest movement among them. It was unclear whether her distance from the sound brewed more relief or anxiety in her gut. She gritted her teeth and turned back to the shelves in front of her and Tate's stash of research. Focus, focus. Enough about her own family. *What are you, Tate?*

There were only a few documents referencing Tate's family directly. Another yearbook, this one a few years older, with a bookmark on a page featuring Marion Mulder. A plastic sleeve containing photographs of Marion alongside an expressionless man. A news article about her late grandmother, a paranoid recluse whose body had not been discovered until weeks after her death. This was almost two decades ago; Leo had heard rumors about it in school, but Tate had never met her grandmother, so she never had much to say about it. As the story goes, the grandmother had kicked Marion out of the house without warning. One day she was fine; the next, she was screaming obscenities and accusations, saying that Marion was invoking the devil. So she kicked her daughter out, essentially disowned her, and never left her house again. Rotted in her own paranoia. Turns out that Marion was pregnant when all this happened. Then the grandmother was found dead just a month after Tate was born. Leo dug deeper into the dusty shelves and started taking apart the contents of the lower one.

She pulled out a blank case containing a single disk. Unlabeled but scratched. A couple others just like it. More news accounts of kids getting lost in the woods all around the state. There were no annotations on any of the documents, to her surprise. The notebook that Tate carried around was evidence enough of her doodling habit. Some of the papers she'd pasted in were filled with more of her own ink than that of whatever she had wanted to collect. Leo's head began to ache in the crease between her brows. The side of her hand did little more than transfer the sweat on her upper lip to another part of her skin. Maybe there was nothing here she didn't already know about Tate. The thought made her feel more grounded than she had in weeks.

But, of course, this thought was futile.

As Leo removed another book, only half-paying attention to the title on its spine, a piece of paper fluttered to the floor in front of her crossed legs. It had been tucked in beside the book, loose on the shelf. Every other small clipping like this was carefully taped into a sturdier volume so that Tate wouldn't lose it. This one had to be different. Special.

Hungrily, she snatched up the paper clipping and unfolded it. It was older than others Leo had seen and contained large sections of blacked-out text beneath the heading. The paper had a different texture, the font that of a typewriter, as if the article didn't go to official newsprint and circulation. It was never published, never seen by the residents of Eston, and filed away by some forgotten force. The headline read: HIGH SCHOOL GRADUATES DIE IN CRYPT COLLAPSE, TWO SURVIVORS SPEAK OUT. Below the bolded words was a black and white photo of a sobbing boy and a disheveled girl with wild hair clutching his arm. A crumbled pile of stones lay in a heap behind them, jutting out from under a small hill. It was an oddly familiar scene. She squinted closer at the girl and the boy in the picture, their faces warped by age and anguish. The caption under the photo: *Kenneth White (18) and Ava Bates (18), survivors.*

The world was ringing in Leo's ears.

Her parents had been to the doorway in the woods. Had seen it collapse and kill their classmates.

She wasn't supposed to see this.

She scooped up the scattered pieces of media and shoved them back on the shelf, heart pounding. Then she froze. Deep rumbling pulsations vibrated the metal and the floor, disrupting the dust that surrounded her. A shift in light came from the other side of the bookshelf. Her hands left Tate's stash of cryptic research on the shelf, and she leaned forward slowly, eyes locked between the metal levels. At first, nothing.

A shadow broke to reveal three spots of light—more dust, she thought, just bigger particles. They hovered in place, forming a lazily floating triangle. She raised her hand to swat away the dust. And the three lights blinked like eyes staring back at her.

Footsteps from the adjacent aisle as the lights scrambled away. A draft like a whisper that tried to turn the sweat at the small of her back into ice and brought a haze to her periphery. Leo stumbled into a sprint and gasped for breath, somewhere in the direction of the rusted staircase that led her here. The stacks of books were exponential. Out from between two shelves and into another aisle, and another, and three more. The aisles closed in tighter, extended up to a vaulted ceiling. Her lungs heaved and black spots swam in front of her eyes. Yes, that's the door over there, just run. A breath on the back of her neck . . . get away—

SLAM!

Leo barreled into a body as it exited one of the aisles. A scream tore out of her throat and burned her chest like acid as she tumbled to the dusty floor, landing on her elbow with a sickening crack. The lightbulbs overhead wobbled and made the floor spin. She scrambled away from whatever she'd hit and pushed down the surge of pain ricocheting up her arm.

"Leo!" A voice cut through the veil of panic. She felt a hand on her shoulder and shrunk from it, stifled another scream. "Baby, hey, it's me; you're okay . . . " Leo opened her eyes wide.

Tate knelt over her. Vision still blurry, eyes refusing to focus. But there she was, and she was beautiful. The warm aura that Tate seemed to carry wherever she went was well-suited to the mystery of the library's stacks. A pastel-colored crop top, her wild curls tucked under a red bandana. Sweetness shrouding secrecy. Leo's chin was tilted up ever so gently, and she felt Tate searching her face for any sign of hurt. Her own stare was glazed, fixed on something far beyond Tate's concerned eyes. The gold flecks in their amber were the mirror of the whirling specks of dust illuminated by dangling bulbs overhead. Leo had never loved her more.

Her voice was soft and intoxicating. It took Leo a few moments to realize she'd been asked a question. She blinked, hard. "What were you doing up here?" Then Tate brushed a hand down to the elbow Leo was cradling, prompting a full-body flinch. "I don't think you broke it, but it's gonna be a real bad bruise," she said. Gingerly, Leo allowed Tate to touch around the knob of bone, extending her arm out and back with extreme delicacy. She watched her nod to herself. Then Tate leaned down and pressed the lightest of kisses into the sore spot, which was already turning purple. "Yeah. Let's just go get some ice on that, huh?" Tate pulled the still-dazed Leo up from the floor by her other arm.

"I'm sorry I scared you," she said as she led Leo to the door. It was only a few paces away, after all. "I've never heard you scream like that before."

Leo glanced over her shoulder into the darkness of the stacks, waiting for something to pounce out from an aisle and claim its prey. She took a few quick steps closer to Tate as she closed the door behind them. "So," Tate said, clearly taking note of her skittishness, "you gonna say anything, or are we just gonna pretend that never happened?"

Released a breath she'd forgotten she was holding. Finally, Leo's voice returned. "There's—there was—" What could she say? What had she seen? Had she seen *anything*? "We'll get in trouble," Leo managed as they stepped down the metal stairs.

"For what, being together? Since when has that stopped us?" Tate smirked and tossed the key to the upstairs library to the clerk at the desk. Leo knit her brow and felt the pocket of her jeans. Empty.

The old woman shot a magnified squint at the pair from behind her glasses. "What was all that yellin' up there? Miss Mulder knows this is a library, so I figured you would as well, Miss Bates."

"Just playing a game, Mrs. Annie." Tate smiled broadly. "We'll be quiet next time. You won't even know we're up there."

LEO ROUNDED THE corner of the town center's intersection with ease on her skateboard, and Sebago followed at close range. One of the lone cars out this late might have honked its horn at her, but she barely noticed. Every pair of headlights were the eyes of the black dog, every shadowed tree bent its limbs to steal her away. Sebbie, thankfully, kept her grounded enough to dismiss these thoughts as paranoia.

By the time they reached the Eston cemetery, Leo couldn't venture a guess as to what time it was. They rolled into the grounds and kept on its tarred path amongst the gravestones for as long as they could, the flashlight from Leo's phone guiding the way with desaturated whiteness. It was uncomfortably silent; most of the crickets already starting to die off at this point in September. September in Maine, anyway, where some days feel like summer and others like the first snow is on the horizon. She'd heard that other places would still be consistently in the warmer-toned light of autumn around this time of year, and not beginning the process of sinking into cold, a six-plus-month hiatus of all waking life. Sebago's brisk trot and Leo's wheels, soon followed by her own sneakered tread, felt far too loud.

At the edge of the woods, beyond the grasp of the pavement and the last row of graves, Leo was forced to take a break, kicking up her skateboard. Though the place was thick with night, she recognized it well. The loose path that she and

Tate had taken that summer was just a few yards from the final few headstones of the cemetery. The air was sharp and cool in her throat. Not to mention, her parents' final resting places weren't too far away, only a few rows down from where she stood. Keeping her focus forward rather than on whatever could be looming behind, though, her flashlight stretched as far as it could to penetrate the spaces between the trees, and it could not stretch very far at all. The feeble light was absorbed by the woods just a few paces in.

If Leo allowed herself, she could picture Tate standing there at the mouth of the trees, just close enough for the light to touch her. The crook in her nose, the notebook under her arm. Grinning like a maniac. Then she would take a step backward and be swallowed by the forest. Like a siren beckoning Leo out to sea. She took a deep breath, and Sebago took a grateful seat by her feet, close enough for her ear to flick at the accidental brush of Leo's fingers.

Suddenly, a vast ray of light flared up behind them and grew more concentrated by the millisecond. Her shadow extended upward from her feet into the trees, an unstable outline with too-long limbs glancing off of leaves. A great mechanical roar climbed to a crescendo. Leo whipped around. A pair of car headlights was speeding in their direction, as if not noticing the lack of defined road, and came to a screeching halt just a few feet from where they stood. Leo retreated, and Sebago barked.

The engine did not turn off when the man opened the driver's door. The headlights stayed trained on Leo, even when the man walked out to the front of the car, hands raised in a gesture that was supposed to be akin to surrender. At first, he was featureless as a shadow. Then Leo saw the thin spectacles catch the glare and the now-ruffled shirt, which before had been so calculated and pristine and distinctly *not* Eston. Detective Ander took a few cautious steps closer.

"Leo, I thought you said we could trust each other," he said. The detective's voice was strained.

LET THE WOODS KEEP OUR BODIES

Her face etched its same old scowl, and she raised a hand to shield her eyes from the headlights. "I did. Why are you here?"

"A couple of reasons," he said. Another step forward. "Your aunt called the station. I had stayed back to do more research after you left. Looked through some old files they keep in that shithole excuse for an archive." He yanked at his tie, which was already askew. There were stains of sweat discoloring his shirt. "She said you ran off. I knew you'd come here before she told me that you might have. Also, that research I was doing." Light bounced off the wetness of his face and grinning teeth. "You know you kids have been playing in an abandoned system of catacombs? Yeah, they say it runs right through here, where we're standing. It was erased from most of the town records after a collapse in the nineties that killed a couple of curious kids like yourselves. Big scandal that they tried to cover up. No one was supposed to know about it; hell, no one even knows where the entrance is these days. Made a playground of a sepulcher, you did." His words were jarring and fast, startlingly different than the composed detective she had been interrogated by just a few hours earlier.

The VHS tapes that Tate had kept in her stash in the upstairs library. *CRYPT COLLAPSE, 1995.*

"I'm aware," Leo said, tightening her grip on Sebago's collar. The dog squirmed and growled at the detective. But how much did *he* know about the doorway? She would need to have the upper hand here—or at least pretend she did. "You need to leave. It's not safe here." Hoped she seemed more intimidating than she felt.

"There's rumors, you know." He took a few paces closer to her. She stood her ground. "People are easy to scare. They think this place is haunted."

"No shit, they do." Her arms spread in an incredulous gesture to encompass the space in which they stood. The rows of gravestones ended just a few paces to Detective

Ander's back, behind his car. The same distance separated Leo and Sebago from the mouth of the woods, where their three shadows were cast by headlights, misshapen and inhuman.

Detective Ander guffawed. Veins pulsated blue and purple at his hairline. "Your girlfriend Tate was certainly one of those lunatics who thought so. All that and more. I need to know if you are, too."

"Does it matter?" The woods were a watchful presence at her back that she tried not to think about. The draft at the back of her neck, the snap of a twig that made Sebbie flinch, were merely figments of her own imagination.

"Undoubtedly. This is an assessment of your ability to cooperate with me on this investigation, Leo. The insane cannot be reasoned with." Leo's jaw dropped, but he continued like he didn't notice, as a rivulet of moisture slid down the side of his bestubbled face. "My job here is to find out what happened to one Tate Mulder. That is why I was summoned to the middle of nowhere all the way from Boston. I intend to do my job, if it kills me. So, do you believe your girlfriend? All those theories she kept in that notebook? *Do* you?"

Fear turned over in the pit of Leo's stomach. Something was very wrong.

"I—" she swallowed, then focused hard to regain her composure. Steadied her hands. "I think Tate was right about more things than I gave her credit for."

"That so? Well, I have a theory of my own. *Folie à deux,* you've heard the phrase, I assume? A delusion shared by two people. Contagious unreality, as it were. That's what plagues yourself and Tate Mulder, and it culminated in the latter's untimely death. The girl wrote about it in her notes, for Christ's sake!"

As Detective Ander rambled, Leo found herself reaching for Sebago, whose fur was standing up on end in a prickling mohawk. She sensed that cutting him off now would be a mistake. So she listened as if his words were bleach pouring into her ears. "The increased state of paranoia combined with your own preexisting genetic mental illnesses, and it might as well have been a guidebook for murder, whether intentional or not. Hell, you couldn't even know! The human mind is quite capable of building up walls of amnesia to protect itself from trauma." He must have seen something change in her face then, and grinned. "That's right. Dissociative amnesia; it's a survival mechanism. Make yourself forget the true horror of what you had done, taking the life of your first and only love, so even *you* had no idea. Truly a tragedy for the ages!"

Leo couldn't breathe. Her knees hit the dying grass with a thud, the cemetery and the woods warping around her. It was like a knife through her heart, scraping between her ribs, shredding the beating muscle. That's not possible; it's not real. She loved her. *But what if* . . . She felt her consciousness begin to retreat, seeking shelter in the back of her mind the way it had trained itself to do.

"You *know* it's possible," Detective Ander said with a strain. He gripped the side of his torso with his right hand as if in pain. Suddenly he looked very tired, and slumped with a wince. "With people like you . . . *you* can't even trust your own mind, so how do you expect me to? Just give me the confession I need, kid, and this will all be over. We'll get you help, I promise. We can make a plea bargain to lessen your sentence and get you a professional diagnosis, some real inpatient therapy. You can leave that batshit aunt of yours for good. I know I'm being hard on you right now. I *know* I am. You don't have to forgive me. But I wouldn't have come here if I didn't think that you were a good kid at heart. All you need to do is tell me that you did it. Please let me help you, Leo."

The earth held its breath and waited for her answer.

And, damn it, the chance to end it all opened in front of her again. She could be safe. Fade into the recesses of her own mind, get *out*. Forget all the world's monstrosities she'd learned about and let them stash her away in a padded white room far, far away. Drift within that void forevermore.

Tate would not be there with her, though.

"How . . . *dare* you," Leo said, clenching her jaw until it ached. She fought to concentrate. Sebago went into a frenzy of vicious barks but stood steadfast beside the kneeling girl. She had to speak up over the din, keeping herself grounded. "You see our trauma and dismiss it by calling us crazy. All the shit Tate and I have been through—together and separately—it made us who we are. I was scared of that. But Tate searched for it everywhere she went. She wanted to be stronger and to have all the answers. That scared me too. But I trust her. More than I've trusted anyone or anything in my whole life, and that includes myself. So how dare you look at us and think that we would *ever* hurt each other. Fear doesn't control me like it does you." In the moment she said it, she knew it to be true. This man was afraid of her. A branch up above shuddered, and a single crow's squawk pierced the night.

The detective removed his hand from where it clutched his ribcage. It came away glistening red, the dress shirt beneath slicked to his body. Leo watched in horror. He groaned then, half-agonized and half-frustrated, and reached behind his back. A gun was aimed straight for Leo's chest, the hands holding it trembling violently.

She scrambled backward, toward the woods and away from Sebbie, who would not follow. The cold ground scraped her palms as she pushed herself to her feet, now hyper-alert. Every movement she made was blurred, in orbit around the sharpened waver of the gun in his hands. "Hey, hey! What the f—"

The man finally broke. "She's *dead!*" Detective Ander bellowed, voice cracking. His stare was unblinking, glasses set aslant. More branches moving over her head, more crows observing the commotion. "You think you can survive with the knowledge she had? It killed her! The monsters we live with, that damn door in the woods . . .

and you *believe* her now . . . " He doubled over, the blood from his chest seeping into the beginnings of a puddle around his feet. Still, the gun was trained on Leo.

Her mind reeled, struggling to comprehend his words. "The door? What do you—" She studied his wrenched expression down the barrel of his gun.

Then she remembered and understood. She believed in what Tate knew. Weird things happen sometimes. And earlier that night, Leo had faced the black dog. The harbinger of an inevitable death on the part of the seer.

This is where she would die.

"What's . . . happening," he grunted. The pool of blood below him was spreading unnaturally fast. As Leo watched in horror, the man's chest bulged at the source of the bloodstain, and he released a guttural scream. She heard the crackle of bones and the splitting of tissue. Sebago's barks turned to feral, bestial snarls with lips pulled back to the gums. When Leo looked down, the dog's eyes were glowing an alien orange.

The world stopped turning, and all was slow. Detective Ander's chest exploded in a wet flurry of blood and organs, but his screams continued to carry, bouncing off the trees and the gravestones. Blood splattered Leo's face, hot and slick. A gaping hole was left in the middle of the detective, ribs jutting out in splinters which he stared down at in shock. Something flinched and writhed about inside his chest, and he wailed. The sound split Leo's eardrums.

A slimy, leech-like creature wriggled its way out from between broken ribs, its swollen body creased against the splinters. Thicker than Leo's forearm and drenched in blood, it fell to the ground in a wet *thump,* and Detective Ander stared in shock. Then other pinpricks of blood on the detective's shirt appeared and spread, bulged at the seams, twisted his body in a grotesque dance. Smaller bursts of tissue revealed more leeches that flopped onto the grass and wriggled into the underbrush. A handful slithered out of his mouth, drowning out his ceaseless throaty screeches, the tail of one leech dangling from a nostril, one leaving a trail of blood from his ear. He heaved, and more came up to splatter below.

Before Ander could take a staggering step toward Leo, Sebago broke from her attention and lunged forward, an unrecognizable canine silhouette hulking and massive against the car's headlights, jaws extended. Claws met oozing leech flesh first, pinning the largest of them to the ground while monstrous teeth ripped it in half with a snarl that was unlike anything Leo had ever heard. Sebago pounced with rippling, misshapen muscles, grown to triple the size. The animal's dripping fangs sunk into the man's neck and thrashed him from side to side with impossible strength, body flailing like a ragdoll. Detective Ander went silent, keeping his death grip on the gun as he was bludgeoned.

Sebago threw him onto the ground, the sheer force clenching his hand. The gun went off with a deafening shot, and Leo collapsed.

BEFORE

"**WHAT THE FUCK** was that?"

Leo lingered behind Tate as the pair left the library and glowered at the back of her head. Tate swiveled around and shrugged, reaching into the pocket of her jeans to reveal a half-crushed pack of Marlboro cigarettes. "I don't know what you mean, babe." Her long fingers picked one out fluidly and placed it between her lips. "Still got that lighter, by any chance?"

"Tate." Heat rushed to Leo's cheeks. "I found your stash up there. I looked through it."

"And? What do you think? You make it sound like I'm hiding drugs in the library archives or something." The last sentence was spoken with a smirk. She held the cigarette between her fingers, then stepped close enough to Leo that she could feel her breath. Her movements were slow and sensual, the smell of her shampoo sweet with coconut. This proximity had been taken away for weeks now, and the nonchalance of it now was staggering. Unbeknownst to Leo, a hand reached around to her back pocket and swiped the lighter she kept there. Tate stepped away and flicked it up to her mouth before Leo could do anything and continued walking toward her car.

Stunned for a moment, Leo bit her tongue, then darted in front of Tate, and stood between her and the driver's side door. "I think this is going too far. I think you're getting obsessive." Tate's eyes gleamed, lit from below her chin by the small flame dancing around the tip of the cigarette. She was a study in defiance, the slight fiery glow on her face enough to give Leo pause. It was a dare to question her further. I'm an open book, but you won't want to know the things I do, it said. Go on and ask; see where it gets you. See if you like it. Tate took a puff and tossed the lighter back to Leo, who caught it without breaking eye contact.

It was a dare that Leo was all too ready to take.

"Why are you collecting those things about my parents?"

Tate blinked. She wilted like a sick rose. "You're the most interesting urban legend of all, Leo. You can't blame me for wanting to know all about you, and everything that made you who you are. Now let me get in my car, please." It was like she'd rehearsed it. Her hand reached for the handle by Leo's hip.

"Hey, wait. I deserve to know *why*."

"And I just told you. Because I love you and want to understand you. Isn't that what you want to hear?" Tate's tone was dismissive, underlined with an eye-roll. It caused Leo's stomach to drop like she was falling and falling, a pain that she had never felt before.

"No. No! Don't do that. It's not just about me." She snapped, then took a deep breath. "The door in the woods." Suddenly Tate's expression changed, and she considered Leo with lowered eyelids. Leo knit her brow and straightened her posture. "Tell me what it is and why my mom and dad were there."

The corners of Tate's full lips twitched into a crooked half-smile. She tucked an escaped strand of hair behind Leo's ear. "Finally, you're asking the right questions." A nod toward the passenger's side of the car. "Get in." Leo didn't hesitate. Tate sped them out of the library parking lot without further comment, and Leo was silently thankful that she'd walked there.

The route they followed was meandering. Back roads that hadn't been repaved in at least a decade or two, pocketed by long-avoided frost heaves and yellow lines faded by the summer sun. Tate was driving just to drive. Just to create that in-between space where conversation could begin and die, all without the need for eye contact. Leo knew the tactic well; she may as well have invented it. So she waited. Tucked one leg up on the passenger's seat and prepared herself for Tate's words which would unravel an untraveled ribbon of road in front of them and lead them further into the unknown.

It took Tate a few minutes to speak. The smell of tobacco permeated her car, and she tapped the ashes of her cigarette out of the cracked open window with a vacant stare. Eventually she shook her head as if to clear it and rubbed one eye. "So, the door," she said. "It's sort of, uh . . . my personal project, I guess you could say. There's not a lot of research I could find on other doors like it. I need to know what it is and what it does. I have a working theory, but it's sort of a lot to take in."

Leo bit back a harsh retort and wanted to beg the girl to not be vague for just one minute, for once in your life, would you? Instead, she chewed the inside of her cheek. "Is it not just access to the underground of the cemetery? I mean, I've never heard of Eston's cemetery having a crypt, but that seems like the most plausible explanation. You said that yourself when we went there. Your notes called it an 'entrance.'"

"Yeah, and then we *went* there, and something happened. You saw." Tate put out her cigarette, now only a butt, on the car's dashboard with the last syllable. It left a smell of burning plastic in the air. Leo glanced sideways and opened her own window. "You looked through the stuff I keep in the library archives, yeah? Did you see the tape labeled '*CRYPT COLLAPSE, 1995*'?" She nodded. "And you watched it, right?"

"I didn't want to take my chances watching it and getting cursed to die in seven days, so no, I didn't watch it."

Leo was pleased to catch the slightest of grins lift Tate's face out of the corner of her eye. "I love *The Ring*. But it's just a recording of an old news segment that ran after that happened. I copied it onto a blank VHS tape I found in the library. Tapes are dope as hell, by the way. We should bring those back." The old light was creeping into Tate's voice, and Leo sighed with relief. "I'd never heard about any of it before this. I think the town tried to cover it up—all the broadcasts and newspapers that reported on it in '95 were pulled from circulation after just a day or two."

"Tate, come on." Her annoyance was becoming harder to conceal. "What is '*it*' you're talking about?"

"The crypt collapse! Listen to me." Tate ran a nervous hand through her curls as the car rounded a tight corner on one of the back roads of the town. They rumbled over a crack in the pavement. "In 1995, a group of high school seniors—including your parents, they were all in a band together or something—went for a walk. That's what they called it. A walk in the woods behind the cemetery, as one does." She said this last part with a tinge of venom, and Leo had to restrain herself from noting that the two of them had done much the same thing.

Something pulled at her attention. "Their band, you said?" The photo from the library stash flashed through her mind, and she pulled it up on her phone. She pointed to the other two kids, a boy on drums and a girl caught singing mid-note, on stage with Ava and Kenneth. They were beautiful, really—trapped in a fraction of a second, the portrait of teenage ephemerality. Leo pointed to them, swallowing against the dryness of her mouth. "The four of them?" Tate glanced away from the road for a split second and nodded.

"Bryce and Mackenzie Talbot are the other two, they were twins," Tate confirmed. "It was them and your folks. Took me a while to find those names. So much of this was covered up. Only recently figured out that the pieces I found were talking about *our* doorway. The kids wandered into the woods the summer after their graduation and found the door. Went inside. Probably to get high. And then it collapsed on top of them for no reason, with no warning. Ava and Kenneth were the only ones who got out alive."

"They survived the collapse," she said to herself. "And then they died, years later." Leo kept the image up on her phone, studying the faces contained there. If she let her eyes lose focus, she could see her own reflection in the glass screen, dull and flat against the artificial LED light. Light wasn't quite the word for it, though—the photograph itself was high contrast in that old film fashion, dominated by shadows that framed the teens during their perpetual performance. But those shadows needed light to be seen. "Darkness Visible," she said.

Tate slammed on the brakes, tires screeching against the withered road. Leo yelped as the seatbelt yanked her collarbone. Tate stared at her with an intensity that was frightening, not dissimilar to the feeling of an actor in a movie that stares its audience in the eye. "What did you just say?"

"Jesus. That was the name of their band. That's all."

"What was?"

"Darkness Visible."

Their gaze was held for a beat too long, and Tate slowly sunk back into the driver's seat. A hand raised to her mouth, and she bit her nails. She resumed driving with a mumbled echo of the name.

Leo's heart pounded. "Why is that—"

"And you *saw*," Tate cut in as if she hadn't spoken. "When we were there, we opened it again. I figured someone rebuilt it after the Talbots died in there. But then it fell . . . again. Before I could even get inside. I *looked* in, though. And all I got from it was two words that made no sense. They came into my mind out of nowhere, didn't see them, didn't hear them. Just *felt* them." She cursed and swerved the car around so they were heading back in the direction of the town center. "We need to go back."

Her mind reeled. *CRYPT COLLAPSE, 1995.* It was that very same door in the woods that she and Tate had gone to see. Or, rather, that Tate had dragged her along to see. It had collapsed and almost killed her parents. The door, the crypt, was town property, and it makes sense that it would be rebuilt after the accident. But then it fell again. This time on them.

Leo felt as if every muscle were paralyzed. She couldn't grasp her own thoughts. "Is the door . . . regenerating?"

"I don't know," Tate muttered. "I don't—ugh." The car swerved into the intersection at the center of town. Horns blared behind them. They turned into the driveway of the cemetery without a blinker.

People always talk about a fight-or-flight response. But what about when the two impulses collide? Primal fear making the skin itch and muscles jump, with animalistic anger keeping a steady gaze and hands curled into fists. It strips a person down to the core of their being—a beast trapped in a prison of flesh. Unable to move. Not fighting or fleeing, but frozen.

The car skidded to a rumbling stop at the end of the pavement road down the middle of the cemetery. Tate jerked it into park, ready to burst out the door, but then paused in her haste and eyed Leo. The girl was staring straight ahead, down the dirt footpath that acted as a continuation of the road to the mouth of the woods. Her heart formed a lump in her throat. If she just stayed there in the passenger's seat, she would be safe. They could forget about the door, forget about her parents. Leave the woods far behind.

A hand slid onto Leo's thigh. Nerves prickled beneath Tate's warm touch. Finally, Leo looked her in the eye and waited for her to speak. "I know you're scared. I'm scared too," Tate said, voice low and smooth. A deep breath was audible in the quiet of the car. "There's something more going on. Yeah, I think the door in the woods regenerated somehow. After Darkness Visible went inside, and the

Talbot twins died, but your parents survived. The door was intact when you and I went back there, as if the original '95 collapse didn't happen at all. And I had never heard that name before, Darkness Visible, but it came to me there. Then it almost collapsed on *us*. So if we go back now . . . "

"Maybe it regenerated again," Leo finished.

"Exactly. We have to test our theory." Tate planted a kiss on her cheek and then opened the car door. "Let's go."

They got out and began the trek into the trees beyond the headstones. Goosebumps rose on Leo's arms, but she kept up pace beside Tate. A twig snapped at the opening between the great oaks at the forest's mouth as they entered.

The walk was wordless, until they drew closer to the doorway, that is. As soon as the telltale mound in the forest floor was within eyeshot in the distance, the air picked up a sort of tension, and made the girls' movements feel sluggish and heavy. Tate's theory turned over and over in Leo's mind, itching like a spider down the back of her shirt. If she was right, if the stone door had rebuilt itself from the shapeless rubble they had left it in, what would they do? What *could* they do? She was sure that Tate—thorough to the point of obsession—must have considered this. She must have a plan. Did Leo *want* to know what that may entail? As they approached the shadowed hillside and just began to make out the doorframe, Leo stopped in her tracks. Tate looked over her shoulder. "What? It's right up there," she said.

"I know." Leo gripped her arms around herself. "Tell me what it is."

Tate hesitated, shifting her weight. As if making up her mind, she nodded to herself and met Leo's gaze. Against the backdrop of the woods, the looming hill creating a darkened aura for her outline, Tate looked like one of the cryptids she was so consumed by. The hybridization of a woodland nymph and a devil, a soft face filled with promises of wonder and whimsy coupled with a certain fire behind the eyes that laid waste to every unlucky lost traveler in her path.

"I don't know for sure. And it sounds fucking insane, I'm aware. But I think the door is a kind of pocket dimension." Leo could feel the matter-of-factness in Tate's voice and the weight of her gaze, waiting for any sign of incredulity or distrust. She didn't have to try to keep a steady expression. Tate continued. "I've read about these places that almost force you outside of yourself because they feel so surreal. It can trick you into thinking you're dreaming. They're naturally occurring, and actually pretty common, since they're really just a gathering point for manifested superstition. You ever been to an empty parking lot at, like, three in the morning, and there's no one else around in a place that's usually so busy, but you feel like you're being watched—and everything is muted, and it's almost like you're . . . watching yourself?" Leo's lips parted. Of course, she knew the feeling. It followed her wherever she went.

Tate took her attention as an affirmative. "There's not one specific word for these places as far as I know, so I've just been calling them black holes. They're weighted points in the fabric of space and time, like black holes in outer space. Except the black holes here on earth are manifested by people's fears and superstitions. Stay with me here. Weaker ones are fairly common, like I said. It's just the most powerful ones, the rarest and heaviest points, which end up being the center of a pocket dimension. I think that's what we're dealing with here in the woods behind Eston's cemetery. That is, if it is indeed regenerating itself. That would prove it as a naturally occurring phenomenon that can heal itself just like any other organism." For the first time, Tate's gaze wandered, and she kicked at the leaves below. "Does that, er . . . does that make sense?"

Here was the girl who was well-liked by all, who had a loving mother, a sizable house, great grades, and a smile for the damned, and of all people, she was asking Leo for validation.

"Yes, it does. I believe you. I mean it." She walked forward and ran a hand down Tate's arm, twining their fingers together. Tate visibly eased the taut cords of her muscles. She hung her head, and Leo still had to go up on her tiptoes to kiss her forehead. "Alright. Let's go see this thing. And whatever we find there, it's gonna be fine, proven theory or not. Got that?" Tate nodded and tucked a loose curl behind her ear. Hands grasped tight, they picked a cautious path closer to the hillside and waited for their eyes to adjust to the shadowed earth where the doorway would make its home. This would be the penultimate moment—before they turned back the way they'd come, quiet with relief and resignation, or before they were confronted with the inarticulate strangeness of the world which Leo had been running from her whole life.

She was reminded of one of the first pages she had seen of Tate's thick notebook. It was a crude, rushed map of the cemetery grounds and the woods surrounding the far pole. An *X* resided near the top edge of the page, deep into the scribbles denoting woods. The very first sign of Tate's black hole theory. It had been labeled "entrance."

And oh, how entranced they were.

Embedded in the hillside was a wall of stone blocks, taller than both of them. In the middle sat withered wooden planks nailed together with iron. The door loomed in front of Leo and Tate with the menace of a guillotine. Unbroken and untouched, as if it had sat undisturbed for a century.

AFTER

THE GROUND WAS cold against Leo's cheek, blades of grass leaving imprints on her skin. Much longer, and they would start to feel more like paper cuts. The gunshot left the mouth of the woods muffled and hazy.

I'm bleeding. A sticky substance weighed down her shirt. She kept her eyes closed and remained motionless, taking inventory of her body. Two arms, two legs, all fingers and toes present and accounted for. Hardly any pain, somehow. Heart pounding. The peripherals of her vision were coated in a thick layer of unreality—the headlights of the car far too bright when she blinked, the stars in the night sky too silver, a shadow's movements too deliberate. A strange crunching was slowly made audible to her adjusting ears.

She pushed herself to a sitting position with trembling arms. The front of her tee shirt was soaked and hung from her body with a sickening weight. Scoured her arms, her torso for bullet holes—until her gaze settled on a misshapen heap in the grass. The blood was not her own. Detective Ander—or what remained of him—lay a few feet away. He was nothing more than a mass of meat and bone just beyond the cemetery, a perch for the curious crows. Swollen bodies of leeches writhed between the weeds. The mangled corpse was backlit by the white headlights which caught all of its grotesque angles and slime.

A wave of nausea and claustrophobia engulfed Leo. Every inch of her skin that was plastered with the gore screamed as if on fire. Erupting out of her daze with a shriek, she clawed at the drenched shirt and left scratches on her skin in the process. The sound of wet shredding fabric cut through the air as she ripped it off in hysteria, chucking it as far as she could and gasping for air. The white ribbed tank top underneath was stained, but at least it was not able to be wrung out with the detective's blood and organ matter. Everywhere she turned provided new horrors; dangling strands of hair clumped in a thick film of liquified tissue. Shoved it out of her face with a retch. She brushed her hands up and down her limbs in a hyperventilating frenzy to get rid of any leeches and didn't find any. Wrapped her arms around herself tightly to ward off the shaking.

Her arm stung with the feverish movements, hot to the touch. Not a bullet hole, but a graze, slick and tender at the peak of her shoulder. A few inches to her right and the bullet would have gone through her throat, all the precious arteries locked there like a fortune. But she was alive for now. Fingers wandered to the pulse in her neck and pressed down hard against its quickened drumming to convince her of the fact.

"S-Sebbie?" she called into the dark. Her own voice hurt her ears.

The barely noticeable crunching sound stopped abruptly. And the silence was worse. The crows beside the corpse went still. One lifted its head, glared at her, had a tendril of flesh dangling from its beak. They were eating the detective.

A larger shadow then peeked out from the other side of the car and emitted a familiar whine.

Relief brought on a deep exhale. "Sebbie, come," Leo said. She clutched her knees up to her chest, eyes fixed on the black birds as they resumed pecking at the scraps of the man.

The canine silhouette lumbered out from behind the vehicle, and all the color drained from Leo's face. It was hunched, hulking, feral. Not Sebago. *What sharp teeth you have, what bulging anatomy and glowing streetlamp eyes. What insurmountable dread you bring with every step.*

All the better to kill you with, my dear.

The black dog had finally come to fulfill its prophecy.

But then it started to change. Leo could do nothing but sit in terror-stricken awe as the monster morphed and shrunk upon its approach, groaning and snarling with exertion. Bones creaked and cracked into a different, smaller shape. The squelching sound of shifting organic framework. Its eyes lost their supernatural glow and dulled. Muscles warped and rippled under the skin and fangs shrunk. In a few moments, she recognized Sebago. The dog's ears were flattened to her head like an admission of guilt, and she lowered her limping body to the ground a cautious distance from Leo, head bowed in surrender.

Leo didn't move. What else had she read about the myth of the black dog? A portent of death, a specter, or a demon . . . *"Some are shapeshifters!"* Tate's eager voice echoed through her mind. They were sitting in the library, early in the summer, going over Tate's most recent discoveries. *"And they're not all so sinister. There have been a few documented cases in New England where a huge ghostly dog had purportedly guided lost hikers back onto the right forest paths at night. Some guarded campsites from bigger dangers. All these monsters and urban legends . . . they're not all something to fear."*

Slowly, warily, Leo went a pace closer on all fours and reached out a hand. The softness of Sebago's brown and black fur, like the plushest of blankets between her fingers. Warm and familiar. More home than her aunt's house. She sighed, and the dog crawled closer to lick her master's knee. "Good girl," Leo whispered.

Her body felt more weighed down and foreign than it ever had to her before, but Leo rose to her feet. The crows were heedless and continued their macabre feast. With each sound of a beak pecking bone, a shiver traced Leo's spine. She needed to leave here before the detective was missed. Get into the woods. To the doorway with all its horrors and promises. First, though . . .

She couldn't help but tiptoe over to the detective's truck, as if what was left of him would jerk back to life to catch her stealing and offer another bullet, this one better aimed than the former. Through the window, sitting in the passenger's seat, Leo saw exactly what she had hoped for. The swollen spine of Tate's collected notebook, half-hidden under a jacket. The door was unlocked, and so she swept the coat aside and hugged the book tightly. It ricocheted her own heartbeat back into her ribcage.

A crow landed on the roof of the truck with a metallic warp. The black bead of its eye fixed on her, and the bird chirped through a bloodstained beak. She backed away. Nevermore.

"Come on." Sebago trotted to her side as she kicked up her skateboard and walked through the mouth of the trees without looking back, Tate's book clutched under her arm.

Of all of Tate's dark findings, of all the mysteries of the world, the atrocities that kept humanity running, there was nothing to explain whatever had just happened. People will abuse one another, kill one another, and Leo could understand that. She could see how anger left unchecked was like a gun on the mantel. Or a knife behind a back. She'd teetered that edge for years, hadn't she? It's so easy to explain things away—you can rationalize it, chase your own thoughts around in circles until you come up with a solution that pleases you. Her mental illness was hereditary, she had reached a breaking point in her relationship, her grip on reality was unreliable at best. But none of that could explain away the fact that Detective Ander's body had burst into pieces right in front of her, or the leeches that ate him from the inside out. That her own dog could shift into a legendary omen of death. Perhaps it could be dismissed as karma, or God, the universe, poetic justice, substitute in whatever other bullshit you chose to delude yourself with. That's the easy way out, though. Some things simply could not be understood, much less rationalized by a measly human being.

What an infuriating idea.

Leo focused on the sounds of the woods. The crunch of leaves beneath her feet, clicking on her flashlight, Sebago's softer tread to her left side. *I'm here, I'm real, I exist*. She felt the old book under her arm, heavy and unapologetic. The taste of the night on her tongue, her own harsh breathing, the sweat on her brow. This is real and happening. She needed to find Tate.

>>>>><<<<<

Of course, of course, the door was perfectly intact when Leo arrived. As it had always been, heedless of the collapses it had been through, uncaring and defiant.

Sebago had slowed from her brisk trot as they approached the structure, and Leo wondered what the dog made of such a strange place. The black dog, rather. Perhaps there was a kinship there, a cryptic entity and a hotspot for surreality, a source of the uncanny. She rested a hand on her dog's head and Sebago leaned into the pat, turning her snout away from the door as if it was painful to look at.

Leo ran her finger along the edge of the pages bound into Tate's notebook, many of them uneven and bloated from the seam. The doorway in the woods, the black hole, waited before her. An ambient roar came from behind its stony entrance, which Leo initially thought was only the nervous ringing in her own ears. She dropped her skateboard on the damp forest floor and raised her phone's flashlight to the frame of the door, casting the strange thing in an undead white light.

Like a black and white photo. Or like someone turned the color saturation all the way down. The door seemed to suck all life from its surroundings. A collection of all the dark parts of Leo's being, a black hole. The stone was crisscrossed with the harsh shadows of branches and leaves that distorted and shifted with Leo's unsteady hand holding the phone flashlight. It was as if the door was overlaid by its history; Leo could feel its connection to the past, sense its memory of crumbling to the ground, its hunger for the blood of all who crossed its threshold. Including Leo and Tate, who had merely stood abreast its entrance—like it was desperate. Starving. Sensed the blood of Ava Bates running through Leo's veins, one who escaped, and *had* to have her.

Sebago whined at Leo's side. She blinked, hard, and shook her head, holding on to the dog's fur to ground her. It was coarse and sticky with dried blood. *Don't think. Stay here. Stay present.*

The thick book opened with a multilayered crinkling sound. Leo held it under the light of her phone, scanning through the pages as quickly as she could under the gaze of the door. What she was looking for, exactly, she did not know. Tate had filled this book to the brim with information of all things unexplainable. There would be something more here that Leo could use to bring Tate back.

It did cross her mind that she would almost definitely flip past the gruesome pages concerning her parents' deaths, but in this moment, Leo did not hesitate. When she came to a modest illustration of what looked to be a spiraling galaxy, black and blue ballpoint pen strokes coming together in freehanded uniformity, she paused. Tate's usual scribblings wrapped around the drawing and filled up the entire following page. It was an unassuming spread, considering the often-unsavory contents of the rest of the book. But the bigger block letters drawn in the upper margin gave Leo pause. *LIMINAL SPACES.*

Leo traced the spirals of Tate's little galaxy with the tip of her index finger. A liminal space at the boundary of what was real and not real, of what was Eston and what was outside, what was unexplainable . . .

An earsplitting series of barks erupted from Sebago. Leo stumbled. The doorway roared and opened.

Just a crack, but that was more than enough. The dark on the other side of ancient wooden planks was somehow deeper than the night. The rustling of the forest fell silent save for Leo's heartbeat. She gripped the open book tight to her chest, held the phone's flashlight in front of her, and started walking. Sebago growled from behind her, tail between her legs. The dog's eyes were beginning to glow a haunting amber. "No, it's okay, Sebbie," Leo whispered. "You can stay out here. I'll be right back." The dog huffed. "I *will*," she repeated. Sebago took a few anxious steps backward, not taking her eyes off Leo. No turning back now. She steeled herself and put a hand on the ancient door.

It opened much easier than Leo was expecting; she barely had to pull at all, and it slowly swung just wide enough for her to walk through. The temperature dropped by twenty degrees the moment she stepped beyond the frame and sent a cold shock down her spine. The white light from her phone illuminated rough, rocky walls and drooping tree roots from the ceiling of the cave.

"Shit." Quickly and without letting go of the door, she reached her foot back to hook her shoe around the nearest upturned track of her skateboard and pulled it forward, wedging it within the doorframe. At that moment, the door became insurmountably heavy and shoved Leo inside with a creak. It caught on the skateboard and left an inch or two of space back open into the woods. The cave almost rumbled in dismay around her. Leo smirked.

Her small triumph was short-lived. Ahead of her, the cave was a sore throat, the walls rough and cracked, leading down into some resentful stomach. The extent of what exactly this cave had swallowed in the years and days before, Leo could only speculate, but knew that it was tied to her. First, it had killed her parents' friends, then it had haunted them until their deaths, and now Tate was undoubtedly locked somewhere in its domain. It was up to Leo to find her before she was digested by the woods. And then Leo would destroy this place.

Her phone's light was absorbed only a few paces ahead of where she stood. She whistled, and the sound bounced around through the cave for what seemed like miles. A shaky breath, and then she started walking.

These were abandoned catacombs, Detective Ander had said. The air was stale and humid, and it was easy to imagine the tunnels stretching on forever, twisting and turning with no discernible destination. No mind for its history of collapses.

There was no indication of distance or time she spent walking deeper into the crypt. All looked the same; dirt, rock, roots. Hours or years could have elapsed until finally something changed. Thin white scratches scored the left side of the cave. Leo almost passed them by without a second glance. Her phone's flashlight caught the edge of the first scratch, and it formed a letter. Then a word, then two. Leo stepped closer and traced the scratches with her fingers. *DARKNESS VISIBLE*. And below that: *1995*.

LET THE WOODS KEEP OUR BODIES

BEFORE

AVA BATES HELD the boy's hand as they trailed behind Bryce and Mackenzie. The twins were vague about where exactly they were taking them, but they'd promised it was a cool little hideaway, prime for getting away from that particular Eston mundanity. They giggled up ahead, Mackenzie shoving her brother, and him almost tripping over a tree root. Bryce shouted with indignance and Mackenzie guffawed.

Kenneth looked over at her, squeezed her hand. "What're you thinking about?"

Ava trailed a hand up his arm and exhaled. She averted her gaze from the twins. In truth, she was ashamed to say that she was jealous of them. Her older sister would never play around with her like they did, would never show that much obvious adoration for a sibling. Deborah was headstrong, whereas Ava was sensitive, and it was exactly that sensitivity that would piss off Deb. All in the hopes of making her stronger, all with good intentions, Ava knew, but what she would give for her sister to show her love just a little bit differently.

She cleared her throat. "The talent show," she said to Ken with a smirk.

His hazel eyes lit up. "Dude, it was *months* ago, and I still feel like I'm floating. That was incredible! The looks on everyone's faces!"

"We came out screaming shitty Nirvana mashup covers; I'm sure the proper blue-pretending-to-be-white-collar citizens of Eston were absolutely mortified. I really hope they saw that Kurt Cobain sticker on your bass! 'Vandalism: beautiful as a rock in a cop's face.' Pure poetry."

"You guys on that talent show again?!" Mac whipped around, her long blonde ponytail draped on her shoulder as she walked backward. "We're graduates now. No more talking about high school. Done with that shit."

"Damn right," Bryce chimed in from up the path. "By the way, we have arrived at our destination. Please put your seats in the upright position and prepare for liftoff." He pulled a joint out of his pocket with a wink. Mac ran up to meet him, scoffed, and snatched it out of his hand, mumbling about how that sentence made no sense at all, and he wasn't even high yet.

Ava and Ken picked up their pace and stood next to Mac and Bryce at the crest of a small hill. Before them stood what appeared to be a manmade mound in the woods, and lodged at the front was a thick stone frame with an old wooden door.

"So you brought us to a crackhead hobbit house to get high, got it," Ava said. Ken snickered and buried his grin in her hair shyly.

"Hey, easy, Bates." Mac leaned against the stone. "This here's an ancient relic. We've never been inside before, but it's the perfect spot."

"Spot for what, just smoking? How riveting." Ken's soft words told Ava that he was only half-joking.

The Talbots didn't take the hint. "That, *and*," Bryce said, "it'll be the final resting place of Darkness Visible."

Ava stiffened, and Mac gripped onto the door's iron handle, leaning back and pulling with all her strength until it creaked hardly an inch. "Uh, what?" The other side of the door was dark, impenetrable already, although it was barely ajar.

"We're leaving," Bryce said. "I mean, Mac and I are going off to Boston for college next week. Finally getting out of this place. We just thought one last dumb romp trespassing through town property was in order."

Ken relaxed, which eased the tension in Ava's hold on his callused hand. "Oh. That's kinda sweet, actually," he said.

"Call me 'sweet' again, and Ava will have to rip me off you, Ken." Bryce blew a kiss and turned to join his sister in pulling open the heavy door, grunting with the effort.

A teasing smile from Ava tilted up to match Ken's blush, and he covered his face in his hands for a moment. When he dropped them, he was grinning, too.

Ava found herself, inexplicably, wanting to cry. The four of them together were losing time; Bryce and Mackenzie would go to some prestigious Boston school on merit scholarships (together, of course), and here was Ava and Ken, whose next big life steps were limited to getting full-time shifts at the mall. The Talbots were leaving Eston. And leaving Ava and Ken in the dust.

The doorway screeched open, and Mac nearly fell. "Phew!" Bryce exclaimed, brushing off his hands on his denim jacket laden with buttons, patches, and zippers. He pulled another joint from his pocket, and Ava wondered how many he had in there. He held it between his lips and lit it. "Let's do this." Mac bounded through the stone doorway with a *woohoo!* and the rest of the band followed.

The tunnel was rough and unkept, smelling of damp forest floor and earth. Their footsteps echoed slightly, and their path was visible only by Bryce's lighter and a small flashlight that Ken always had fastened to his car keys. The Talbots had come unprepared and overly enthusiastic, as per usual. The daylight from the open doorway behind them grew smaller and smaller until it was merely a pinprick, and they rounded a corner.

"What is this place, anyway? Did you figure that out, at least, before you brought us on another trespassing adventure?" Ava took a drag.

Mac chuckled. "Er, not really. Our best guess is that it's connected to the cemetery."

"How'd you find it?" Ken looked uneasy, focusing his flashlight on cracks in the rock while they walked.

"We just—" Bryce grasped for words.

"Sensed something out here, last week," Mac finished. "The same feeling you get when someone is staring behind your back." He shrugged. "Wanted to give it a closer look with you guys. Could be a new secret hangout spot."

"Weird." Ken glanced backward at Ava and stopped. No one acknowledged that soon half of them would not be around to hang out. "I think this is far enough," he said.

"Okay," Bryce said. He handed a pocketknife to Ava, blade unsheathed. She took it slowly, questioning him. He nodded to the wall of the tunnel. "You do the honors, frontwoman. *Here lies the greatest band in the history of Eston, Maine.*"

"We're not dying," Ava said. "Just moving on." Nevertheless, she inscribed on the stone: *DARKNESS VISIBLE, 1995*. The other three watched in silence as she did so.

They sat in that stone tunnel for an hour, chatting, reminiscing. Smoke drifted from their mouths and noses, with wicked, smoldering smiles. They floated in the space between childhood and adulthood, known and unknown. This place was familiar and strange. Blissfully unaware of the horrors they rested upon and all that would come afterward.

It started as a low, imperceptible rumble that could've been Bryce's stomach growling. But the sound grew, deepened, traveled up from the depths of the tunnel, until it was all around them and vibrating the ground beneath their feet. They looked at each other.

Ken was the one who started running first. He'd grabbed Ava's hand and yanked her out of her stupor, the two sprinting back the way they'd come as the ground quaked and the tunnel crumbled around them. Rock and debris fell from the ceiling, drowning out Bryce and Mackenzie's running footsteps behind them. Ava choked on the dust and struggled to keep up, Ken's vise on her arm starting to ache.

Approaching the entrance now, almost there. The daylight from the open door was intermittently broken by falling rock. She heard a cry out from behind her and glanced over her shoulder just in time to see Bryce's sneaker snag on a gnarled tree root, and the boy hit the ground hard. Mac yelled something and turned back. She bent down to help her brother, and before Ava's eyes, the Talbot twins were swallowed and crushed by the collapsing tunnel.

Ken kept his gaze forward. The stone entryway was beginning to shift in front of them, walls grinding and ready to fall. The wave of ruin chased them to the doorframe, clipping their ankles and the backs of their legs. They dove through the door and were hit with daylight and the splinters of the door's wooden panels as they buckled under the weight of debris.

The underground roar of collapse went on and on, and Ava and Ken held each other through the dust and blood as if they each were the only thing keeping the rest of the world tethered together.

AFTER

TEARS STUNG LEO'S eyes as she touched the inscription in her mother's scrawled handwriting on the wall of the tunnel. In that touch, she felt her pain, her grief. Felt the pocketknife in her hand as it scraped against the rock and left white gravestone letters in its wake. She saw the Talbot twins die and felt that crypt collapse haunt Ava for the rest of her days. Waiting for collapse at every moment. She and Ken had survived, until they hadn't. Until the ruin finally caught up to them.

The light from her phone's flashlight glanced at every ridge of the tunnel wall, a harsh topography. When she shone it on the words directly, all went white, and the scratches were drowned out in the brightness. Only when the very edge of the beam met the inscription was it visible.

"It's okay," Leo said. She could see Ava, Ken, Mac, and Bryce running down the tunnel, rock falling all around them. "It ends tonight." Her fingertips brushed the inscription one last time, and she turned away to journey farther into the depths of Eston underground.

The deeper she went, the more the tunnel seemed to morph. Less stone and more dirt, more dangling roots of trees above, more decay. At one point, her flashlight met nothing but darkness ahead of her, unable to touch the ground.

She stepped forward. Suddenly, Leo's stomach dropped out from under her, and she was falling.

All was pitch black save for the whirling flashlight falling beside her. She felt a scream tear through her throat rather than hear it; rushing air whipped her face and burned her skin. She braced herself as much as she could for a bone-shattering landing.

It never came.

When Leo opened her eyes, she was standing in the Eston Public Library.

Except it was different. The towering bookshelves were usually lit by that familiar fluorescent white-yellow glow from the lights above. Now, the library was dark and bathed in a harsh red glare like emergency lights.

The place was abandoned; no old Mrs. Annie at the front desk, no one perusing the aisles of books. There was nothing outside the windows but blackness. Leo was alone. An ambient, chasmic roar underlapped the space. Her hands were the same hue as the floor, the ceiling, the shelves, those red lights canceling out all color variation.

"Hello?" she called over the dull thundering. The aisles of books were laid out in exactly the same manner as the library she knew. Fiction organized in alphabetical order by author, a few smaller genre sections near the walls. A horror section that barely took up a shelf of space and was almost exclusively made up of Stephen King. Her hand trailed along the spines of the reddened books as she walked by. It even smelled the same. Dust and old paper, ink near the printers, cheap coffee. Leo pinched the inner side of her forearm to ground herself.

She knew this place, and she did not. Leo's head pounded at her temples. The red light was discombobulating. There was the front desk, the wheeled cart of returned books, the creaky wooden tables. The table in the back where Tate had sat Leo down that day to introduce her findings. *Tate*.

If Tate was in the library, she would be upstairs, Leo thought, in the archives looking over her collection of town history. She rounded the corner of the last of the bookshelves. The door to the stairway was where it always had been, and it was closed.

Leo was hardly aware of stepping toward the door until her hand wrapped around the handle. She opened it.

Where the stairway to the archives should have been was a darkened room, just out of reach of the red emergency lights in the library. It was familiar. An unmade bed to one side, the moonlight falling in from a window above it cut through over and over by the blinds. The contrast in lighting hurt Leo's eyes. A messy desk at the other end, papers strewn about, and clothes on the floor. A bulging book lay open on the bed, and Leo realized she was no longer holding her own copy of it.

This was Tate's bedroom.

The ambient noise stilled, leaving a ringing silence in Leo's ears. Her breathing sounded far too loud in its absence. She clenched her fists. "Tate?" She hated how her voice shook.

The bedroom was empty. Leo took one slow step inside and felt the plush carpet under her shoes. The door slammed shut behind her with a crash that turned her blood to ice.

"Hey!" She whirled and pounded on the door, but it wouldn't budge, and the knob wouldn't turn. The only evidence of the library beyond was the red light bleeding in through the cracks between the doorframe.

All was dreamlike. If Leo allowed herself, she could believe she was actually there in Tate's room. She turned to the bed, where her notebook rested plainly, daring Leo to take a peek inside. She knew what pages it would be open to without needing to look.

Just as Tate's mother Marion had found it the morning she'd realized Tate was missing, the notebook was open to the spread about the murder-suicide of Ava Bates and Kenneth White.

Leo gritted her teeth. The crime scene photos collected on the pages were oversaturated, too-clear points in the monotone room. The fire of Ava's hair draped over their pale flesh, dark red blood streaming from their wrists.

Kenneth's head resting in her lap in an eternal comforting sleep. And then the photo of Leo herself on the next page, barely ten years old, red-faced and caught mid-scream after she stabbed the policeman who had delivered the news.

She knelt in front of the book, reached around to her back pocket, and felt the crinkle of Tate's ripped-out pages there. She took them out and unfolded them.

When I was a kid, I got lost in the woods behind my house.

It shouldn't have been that easy to get lost, but it was. I was wandering around, thinking about that girl whose parents just died. It was broad daylight. I felt bad for her. I thought about running away.

Next thing I knew, I couldn't see my house anymore. I tried going back the way I came, but I couldn't get out of the woods. The sun set, and I was crying, walking aimlessly, and probably getting myself more lost in the process. Mama was out looking for me, she'd told me later. She got a search party together and everything. It didn't help until I found it.

You know the rest.

I saw something on the ground up ahead. Flies buzzed around a dark heap in the weeds. It looked like an adult taking a nap on the forest floor; they were all curled up and comfortable. My stupid kid-brain wanted a closer look. Maybe they could help me get out of here. So I got closer.

*Among the weeds, a corpse. Maggots where eyes used to be. My eyes. My rotting skin. **I am not the only me**.*

It made Leo lightheaded reading the words in Tate's distinctive handwriting. She smoothed out the folds in the pages. She flipped through the notebook, away from the pages about her parents, until she found the rips near the spine where Leo had torn these pages out. She'd wanted to shield Tate from that vision, that pain. Had seen herself in that trauma and wanted to preserve her from it. So she'd ripped them out behind Tate's back after they'd watched the crypt collapse, hidden them away so she wouldn't have to think about that memory anymore. She wanted to save her from her past, just as Leo was trying to do for herself.

She lined up the rips in the paper with the remnants in the spine of the notebook. They fit together perfectly. Everything in its right place. The papers fused together from the bottom to the top with a sound not unlike shredding paper played in reverse. Leo blinked, tugged on them once. They held strong to the seam. Good as new.

Leo let out a chuckle. "Well, alright then." She closed the notebook and stood up, hugging the volume tight to her chest. She took a deep breath and eased the tension in her shoulders.

BAM BAM BAM. A pounding at the door where Leo had come in. Two shadows broke up the red light from the library, bleeding under the door like feet standing on the other side.

"Oh, fuck." She looked around frantically for a place to hide. The knocking came again, faster, impatient. It shook the bedroom.

"Shit. Fuck. Shit." The closet. She ran and yanked open the slim closet door. Shoved her way between the coats and clothing and shut herself into darkness.

The door to Tate's bedroom, which should have been connected to her hallway, her loving home with Marion, swung open and red light from the Eston Public Library flooded in. A silhouetted being stood in the doorframe, cut through by the horizontal grate of the closet where she hid. Something writhed and pulsated in its middle, wetness reflecting the emergency lighting.

Leo covered her mouth to muffle her heavy breathing. She gripped Tate's notebook until her knuckles turned white.

Detective Ander stumbled into the bedroom, leeches pouring out of his abdomen and chest.

The man was only recognizable by his stature and the cracked spectacles barely hanging on his face. Blood and slime drenched his body; some of the leeches latched on to his skin and sucked hungrily, some inched their way out of the new orifice in his middle, others plopped onto the floor with sickening, wet slaps and wriggling away. The detective grunted a bubbling sound, looking around the bedroom. Looking for Leo.

She dared not move, letting the contents of the closet nearly suffocate her. What used to be the detective lumbered around with a limp. His hand extended, changed, until a tentacle-like appendage wrapped around the bedframe, and lifted it effortlessly, throwing the bed against the wall with a loud crash that sent a shockwave up Leo's spine. The thing groaned as he found nothing of interest underneath.

Leo was powerless. Trapped. She took an involuntary step backward, further into the cramped space. Her foot crushed something below. Something that sounded like a twig snapping in the woods.

Detective Ander's head whisked up, and he stared Leo dead in the eyes.

"*T-th-there-re y-you a-are-re.*" His voice was something between a hiss and a deep, hollow thrumming.

A deafening reptilian howl. It lunged toward the closet and ripped the door off its hinges with tentacle limbs. Leo held up the notebook to shield her eyes.

All went silent.

Her quaking breaths refused to slow. After an eternity, she lowered the notebook and looked around. Darkness surrounded her and the air smelled damp and earthy. She felt her phone in her pocket and took it out, turned on the flashlight. The walls of the tunnel stretched out before her. Under her foot, a twig was broken in half. And behind her, just another dirt wall.

She was somehow relieved to see it all.

This part of the crypt felt different. The atmosphere was thicker. Though it looked much the same as anywhere else Leo had walked through the tunnel, this section was heavier. Perhaps she was getting close. She followed the gnarled tree roots on the ground as they grew closer together, all reaching forward in the same direction. Leo stepped over them carefully.

Eventually, the roots spliced together, growing wider the farther Leo traveled, tangled in natural knots that lined the cave. They would culminate in these protuberances on the floor, the walls, the sloped ceiling. Strange growths seemed to pulse in time with Leo's footsteps. She eyed them and gave a wide berth whenever she passed one. They were like tumors deep within Eston.

She came upon a massive one. It took up the entire width of the cave, nodulous tree roots intertwined into one throbbing cancer. Leo shone her flashlight upon it. A dead end. Helplessness strangled her lungs. The flashlight followed up the thickest of the roots through the center of the growth, where it reached its peak in a spiral.

And there, tangled in the roots of the largest tumor at the ceiling of the cave, was Tate.

"Oh my god," Leo said. Tate was frighteningly pale, her eyes open and white with no warm amber irises. Her curly hair dangled down in a curtain that framed her expressionless face. She was tethered to the tunnel by her arms, torso, and legs. The roots wrapped around her like chains, and she hung there limp.

Leo jumped onto the roots, climbing to reach her. "Tate, hey, I'm here. Wake up, baby," she pleaded. The roots scraped her hands and left splinters in her fingers. Several feet off the ground now, Leo struggled to keep her hold on the roots and the flashlight trained on Tate.

Tate groaned, tilting her head.

"That's it. Come on." Leo took out her pocketknife and tried sawing through one of the thinner roots holding Tate in place.

"L-Leo?" She tensed, starting to squirm under the roots. "I'm stuck," she said. "And . . . I can't see. Where are we?"

Relief flooded through Leo, her eyes filling with water. The pocketknife didn't make a dent in the roots. She put it away for now and held Tate's face in her hands, trembling. "It's okay, I've got you. We're in the black hole. I'm gonna get you out of here."

"The black hole," Tate echoed. Her eyes went wide, all cloudy white. "We have to get out." She thrashed in the tangle of roots. They only seemed to tighten around her. An all-too-familiar roar sounded from deep behind the tumor that trapped Tate. Leo stared into the impenetrable darkness from which she'd come.

"I know. I'm thinking." The knife wouldn't cut. Tate couldn't free herself from the inside. The cave was beginning to collapse again.

"You're *thinking*," she said. "God help us all."

Leo paused for a moment, but then saw Tate grin weakly. A tear dripped down her face, and she laughed once. "I've missed you," she said.

Tate sniffed. "I'm sorry," she replied. "I wanted to know everything about you. But I really never did know you, did I? I only knew what I wanted to. Only the weird stuff that I liked. In some stupid effort to give all of this a purpose. I'm sorry, Leo." She was sobbing now.

"It's okay; it doesn't matter right now."

"No, it does," Tate retorted. "It's the reason we're both stuck down here right now. I've killed us both."

The tunnel rumbled. The tree roots that suspended Tate began to shake, grinding into her skin. Dust and a few pebbles here and there started falling from the ceiling.

"Tate," she said. Time was running out. "You were right, but you didn't know the whole truth."

She coughed. "What?"

"You were right," Leo repeated. "About Eston. There's something very wrong here. I think you knew too much about it, you tried to tell me, and it used that to hurt you."

Tate didn't move. The rumbling grew louder, grew into a roar. "Eston killed the Talbot twins when they were about to leave for college. It tried to kill my parents at the same time, and it failed. So it haunted them, corrupted my mom until she thought *they* were the problem—" she choked, "—until they tried to run away through the woods. They made it to the edge of town. They were desperate. And then it finally overtook them, after years of trying, and they died."

"But not before you had already come along," Tate said.

Leo nodded. She had to shout over the quaking earth now. "You had that vision when you got lost in the woods as a kid because you were thinking of me and wanted to run away. No one is allowed to leave Eston. And I shouldn't have even been here in the first place."

The tumorous tree roots began to shift with the cave's movements. They broke apart with a *crack,* and Leo and Tate fell to the ground. Leo scrambled to pull Tate out of the way of more falling debris.

"No," Tate said, the color slowly returning to her face, her eyes. She met Leo's gaze for the first time as her head rested in her lap. "You're definitely supposed to be here with me."

The wall up ahead crumbled to the floor. Leo's ears popped with the pressure. "Come on," Leo said. In a frenzy, she helped Tate stand up, wrapped an arm around her hip, and held on tight with her other hand to Tate's around her shoulders. They ran. Tate's notebook fell open on the ground in their wake and was swallowed by the collapsing walls of the crypt.

Tate limped against Leo's side, the latter almost dragging her. The bedlam was concentrated behind them; they had time, they would make it out.

Leo's foot caught a gnarled root, and they were both sent plummeting.

It was not the crumbling ground of the crypt that their hands and knees landed on, though. The old carpet of the Eston Public Library rose to meet them, bathed in harsh red emergency lights.

"What the fuck?" Tate coughed.

"Keep going." Leo pulled her to her feet. The roar of the collapsing cave sounded far-off, like music playing in another room. "Gotta find the exit."

Aisles of bookcases elongated to the ceiling as they wove between, redness saturating. The shelves shifted, turned, a living labyrinth. It was some unwritten circle of hell beneath Eston, where the small town's residents would wander in perpetual ennui.

A glowing exit sign came into view around one final corner, hovering over a darkened maw in the place of the real library's double doors. "There." Tate pointed. Leo picked up their pace, tugging Tate along and gasping for breath.

Two figures emerged from the darkness ahead.

Eye sockets were empty voids, limbs skeletal. But they were humanoid—no taller than Leo and Tate, wearing tattered clothing that draped over them formlessly. Despite the red light they were pale and corpselike. One had a leg broken and twisted at a gruesome angle, the other's spine jutting out from mummified skin at the throat. The latter's head was barely attached to its body. A denim jacket, a blonde ponytail.

It was Bryce and Mackenzie Talbot.

"Oh, my god." Leo froze, gripping Tate tighter. The twins hobbled into the library, and Leo braced herself.

Bookshelves exploded behind them, sending volumes scattering across the labyrinthine room. The amalgamation of leeches that used to be Detective Ander writhed towards them from under the carnage. Tentacle-like arms stretched and pulsated, reflecting the red light over the creature's slick body. The thing had no discernable face anymore, covered in parasitic little shapes that gurgled and groaned. A deafening roar as the collapsing crypt made itself known once more, rapidly approaching. They were cornered.

The Talbot twins passed Leo and Tate without regard.

Instead, they met Detective Ander and his multiplying legion of leeches. A tentacle whipped in their direction. Mackenzie caught it out of the air with her sinewy arms, impossibly strong. Her dangling head rocked and threatened to fall off the rotten flesh with the force. The detective creature shrieked as if her touch burned him. Thousands of tiny leeches swarmed up the twins' legs. Bryce's corpse pulled a lighter from his denim jacket pocket, and flicked it as they were engulfed in the swarm.

Flames erupted. The leech-creature howled. Bryce and Mackenzie were lost to the fire and the displacement of air threw Leo and Tate back into the black gap under the exit sign. They hit the ground of the crypt.

Dirt fell in their hair, their faces. Deafening *thud thud thuds* of falling rocks all around them.

"Leo," Tate said.

The wind had been knocked out of her; Leo sputtered, "We have to get out of here." The crypt shook as if in an earthquake, scattering rock and root around them in a violent storm.

And on the other side of the largest knot of tree roots, which now lay broken and half-buried, was the first light of daybreak shining through a crack in the door.

They reached the door and felt its wooden beams hold strong against them. The walls fell inward, shoving them close together. Leo's skateboard was still lodged in the gap between the door and stone, providing a couple inches of space.

"*Sebago!*" Leo screamed through the gap.

Glowing streetlamp-orange eyes met her own.

Sebago the black dog clamped her monstrous jaws around the wooden door and tore the first plank free from its iron bearing.

Tate screamed, and Leo shoved her through the widened gap. Sebago sank her preternatural fangs into the next board and started tugging. It broke in half and left dagger-like splinters behind.

Leo started climbing through the gap in the door. Tate grabbed her hand to pull her through.

The rest of the crypt collapsed in an instant, and Leo fell onto the spiked door plank. She heard the doorway seal behind them with a *whoosh* of air as she was pulled onto the leaf-covered earth, saw the pale morning sky above, and all went black.

BEFORE

THE BLACK HOLE, the strange doorway in the woods beyond the cemetery, stared at Leo and Tate in defiance of nature.

Neither girl could speak. Tate cleared her throat. The door was indeed less haunting in the daylight, but it still felt *wrong,* as if they were looking at a piece of the world that simply didn't belong. Leo felt her consciousness start to drift, her thoughts becoming spaced out and foggy, and she swayed. She grabbed Tate's arm.

"It's alright," Tate said, not taking her eyes off the door. "It's—we knew this could be how it is. This proves it. A pocket dimension . . . a liminal space." She brushed Leo's hand that clutched her bicep and swallowed before speaking. "Can you—can you touch it?"

Leo froze and stared up at Tate, still fighting dissociation. "What?"

"Maybe something will happen," she said. "If you get close enough."

A pause. "Why me?"

"Because. It has to be you."

Leo let out an exasperated sigh. "There's more to that theory you're not telling me, Tate." Her wide eyes blinked in surprise. She opened her mouth to respond, but Leo kept talking before she could lose momentum. The words that tumbled out surprised her. "The reason you need me here with you. You couldn't just come back here alone."

"I just—like I said before, you and your family are at

the center of so much that's happened. The kids that go missing around the place they died, the first collapse, almost everything. Can we not start this right now? We're right here—"

"My parents survived the '95 collapse, and maybe they weren't supposed to. The door lured you in so that I would follow. So it could finish the job. You're testing your theory."

Tate's lips parted. Gaze flickered away. Leo waited for a reaction—a furious rebuttal, an indignant glare, hasty denial, anything. Tate stayed silent and blank. Her mouth almost tried to form words, slowly finding shapes that fell and lost their structure before a voice could fit the mold. Finally, she shook her head slightly, still not looking Leo in the eye. "It's not—it wasn't like that."

"I think it is." First, disbelief froze Leo to the core, waiting for Tate to deny it, and then the warning bubbles of fury churned in her stomach. Her hands folded into tight fists at her sides. They were trembling. "This is all about the fucking door. You care more about proving some insane theory about, what, pocket dimensions and supernatural creatures? You care more about that than my *life,* Tate?!"

"No! God, no, Leo!" Tate's voice broke, and her eyes went glassy. "I'm just trying to understand."

"Understand *what?*" Leo snarled.

Tate flinched. "You," she said in a small voice. "And me. I'm trying to understand who—or what—we are. Why we're here. In Eston."

Leo felt dizzy. She could feel her ire in the pulse of her fingertips. And she could feel that she was about to say something that could never be taken back. She didn't try to stop it. "You don't get to use me to solve your own existential crisis. We are *nothing,* you understand that, Tate? *Nothing.* There's nothing special about me or you or this town. Nothing *unexplainable.* We are specks of dust floating through space, we are biological accidents, we mean nothing, and the very urge to mean *something* is futile because there. Is. *Nothing*. And your obsession with finding proof of otherwise is pointless. You don't get to use me and my trauma to satisfy some neurotic fantasy." As the words tumbled out, she knew it was true. "I can't do this anymore."

Tears filled Tate's widened eyes, spilled over onto her cheeks. Silence. The birds stopped their chatter, the leaves stood still. For the first time, Leo felt a crack split through her unyielding anger, like an earthquake splitting a landmass, sending Richter-scale tremors down her body. She'd gone too far.

Tate just stared at her until Leo had to avert her gaze. "You need to leave." Tate nodded as she said the words and walked forward to place an unsteady hand on the door.

Leo's body ached in a way she had never felt before. Tried to think of something to say, how to take it back, but came up blank.

"You're right. There's no point to any of this. We were made to hurt each other." The door creaked open under her touch. She pulled the old handle, and it opened further. The darkness within was almost hard to look at; Leo's eyes strained to make out anything beyond the stone frame. Tate was outlined by the void at this point, the door fully opened and ready to lure her inside.

"Wait—"

She whipped around with venom in her voice. "*Go away.*" Tate's eyes were completely washed out, not an ounce of warmth, nothing but fogged-over paleness where her dark irises had been moments before. "I said I would rather die anywhere else. Anywhere but Eston. But maybe there is nowhere else."

Leo stared, lips parted. She reached out a hand very slowly. "Tate, step away from the door, please—"

"No." The door behind her started to rumble. "Get out of here, Leo." Instead, Leo took cautious steps closer. Tate straightened, and her face went blank. Leo felt tears run down her jaw. The trees around them swayed and bent. And then Tate said the worst sentence Leo had ever heard, three words that she herself had spat in anger just minutes before but that felt so wrong out of Tate's mouth, four syllables that would scar her heart and echo through nightmares for years to come.

"There is nothing."

Tate was thrust backward. She fell to the ground and clawed at the leaves on the forest floor as she was dragged by an invisible force, past the threshold of the door and into the darkness. She let loose a bloodcurdling scream, and the door slammed shut with a roar that shook the woods and sent the crows scattering overhead. As if the sound had split the sky open, it began to downpour.

Leo ran as if hell itself were chasing her.

Eston was a place of benign familiarity. Sun-faded pavement and a town center that hadn't seen construction in decades. Brick by boring brick, she knew it all. The leaves seemed to fall in the same places every autumn. And this autumn, this dying season in particular, continued on without regard for Leo.

She *had* to know it all. This is where she'd grown up, where her parents had grown up, where they'd died. There couldn't be a corner Leo didn't know, a shadow she didn't recognize. And yet this safe, familiar town had swallowed Tate alive.

In the rainy days that followed, Leo felt frozen in place. Her terror of the woods—there was something in there, wasn't there?—kept her on a strict path from her aunt and uncle's house to school and back, and that was only when she dared to go to school at all. Something was watching her, waiting for her.

The so-called familiarity was overwhelming. Small-town suffocation. But look too closely at the things you know, and they'll become entirely alien. The familiar, however safe and comforting, can be destructive if you stay there too long. That pillow you rest your head on every night can turn around and block the air from your lungs. Your morning walk down the street can end in getting hit by a car with an out-of-state license plate that was never supposed to be there. The familiar becomes strange the longer you look at it, like a word you see over and over again until it loses its meaning. Why did the trees grow where they did, thickest at the edge of the cemetery? Why was Leo's hair the same fiery hue as her mother's? Why did all the lights in the town turn off at the same time? Why did Tate have to be gone, and not Leo? Where had she gone?

When Leo arrived home after that night in the woods, she was silent. She walked to her room with glazed eyes, without acknowledging Aunt Deb, Uncle Mike, or even Sebago. Her guardians had stared after her in confusion, with her knotted hair and the dirt under her nails. Crawled into bed fully dressed, shoes and all, and stayed under the covers until light shone through the fabric and Deb stood over her. Dissociation crept through her consciousness, sped up time, shielded her from what she had seen that night. Tore out the pages and locked them away. "What's wrong? Did something happen to you?" her aunt kept asking. Leo was unresponsive. It was Uncle Mike who finally asked the question as he sat at the foot of her bed, desperate to get her to talk: "Did that girl break up with you or something?"

Leo had shot up out of bed, face red and brow furrowed tightly. Uncle Mike actually flinched, like she was a wild animal snarling in his face. "Don't *ever* fucking say that again. Tate is *gone!*" Leo spat, barely understanding the words as she said them. His eyes went wide, and he just nodded quietly and left. Leo might have felt guilty under different circumstances.

It was maddening. Aunt Deb had questioned her again and again after that. "What do you mean she's 'gone'?

What does that even mean?" Leo hadn't been able to answer.

It wasn't until later that morning, the fifth of September, that Marion Mulder had given them a call to see if Tate was there. Aunt Deb, for once, had seemed speechless. "N-no, she's not here . . . really? And she's not answering her cell phone? . . . I don't know, Leo has been acting strange . . . I think you should call the police, Marion."

The echo of sirens floated down Eston's streets like an unforeseen storm as the afternoon light turned to gold and faded. Heads poked out of windows, people stood out on porches, some more curious souls took a walk down to Tate's house to catch a glimpse of the trio of police cars parked along the road. Shadows of multiple officers flitted through the windows of the house, occasionally paced by the hands-wringing figure of Marion Mulder. At one point, there was a small crowd of onlookers in the driveway, whispering amongst themselves. "I think Marion's girl is missing." "Heard them talking about searching the woods." "Remember this happened when Tate was younger? She got lost in the woods for hours. Guess it's happening again." "She's been hanging out with the Bates kid. Yep, that one."

Leo stood a distance behind the crowd, hands in her thin jacket's pockets. Her throat felt tight as never-ending rain spattered the pavement.

The front door swung open suddenly, and the crowd fell silent. Most of the officers walked briskly out to their cruisers. One stopped before the gathered neighbors. "If you're not here to help, folks, go on home," he muttered. "If anyone wants to assist us in securing the woods in a couple miles' radius, we're gonna be splitting up soon." Most of the gathered audience turned away and scattered. Leo was left exposed.

The officer eyed her. "You need something, kid?"

She flinched and took a step back. "No."

"Actually, hold on." Another cop trotted over from his car. He mumbled something into his radio. "Leonora Bates, right? We'd like to speak with you, if you have a minute—"

"I don't. My aunt needs me home before sundown," she lied. Heart thudding, she turned on her heel and took a few quick steps before letting her skateboard hit the pavement and jumping on, skating behind the trees lining the road and out of sight.

Her mind was a clean slate which she did not—could not—comprehend. All she knew was that Tate was gone. And she was alone again.

AFTER

SOFT MORNING LIGHT, dappled and rosy gold, cast a too-sweet luster over the shriveled leaves littering the ground. The world was impossibly warm and still. Leo's aching head was eased gently in an up-and-down rhythmic breathing, and she realized that she rested on Sebago's flank. If she could go back to sleep, just sleep for a little while longer . . .

Her surroundings slowly came into focus. The browned leaves pocketed by bits of overgrown grass and moss which made up her bed, the ground that sloped into a small hill a few feet away. Not a single great stone, not a splinter of the ancient planks from the door. As if the woods had been smoothed over in the early hours of the day, healed itself of something that hadn't belonged. Her skateboard was broken in half, the second jagged piece nowhere in sight. Where was Tate?

Leo's muscles begged to be stretched, sore down to the bone. But her consciousness surrendered of its own accord as she ran her hand down Sebago's plush pelt and sank back into an exhausted stupor.

It was only another hour or two before they found her like that. A sickly-looking girl curled up half-conscious in the middle of the woods with a dog who snarled and snapped at anyone who got too close to her. The search party was ear-splitting, Aunt Deb's shrill voice cutting above the cacophony of others. She was dimly aware of Uncle Mike coaxing Sebago into a relative calm, while a pair of people shone a light in Leo's eyes and wiped at the dried blood under her nose, the scrapes on her stomach and awful splinters buried there. One muttered something about catatonic shock.

"Did you call that detective from Boston?"

"He's not answering his phone."

"Well, find him."

"His car's not at the motel he was staying at. He wouldn't have left, would he?"

"Better not have. But that's what we get for hiring an out-of-towner."

Soon she was lifted off the ground, and she wanted to scream, to thrash, escape the arms that held her like her life depended on it. She must have done something to that nature then, as the voices around her escalated with the urgency of panic, Sebago's frantic bark sounded from several steps away; there was a quick pinch in her arm, and the woods fell away from her.

The only urgent care clinic in Eston was rarely so bustling and frenetic. Nurses came in and out of the room where Leo found herself resting on a bed with an IV line taped into the crook of her arm. Aunt Deb and Uncle Mike sat in chairs to her right. She was pleased to see Sebago snoozing away on the floor beneath them. "Where is Tate?" she croaked.

Mike sprung to attention a little too fast, and Deb calmly walked over to sit at the foot of the clinic bed. She hovered her hand over Leo's leg but thought better of it and knitted her fingers together instead. "They found her, honey," Deb said.

"So where is she?" Leo demanded. Her abdomen ached as she tried to straighten her posture. If none of that was real, if they'd only found a body . . .

"She's taking it easy," Mike answered.

"She'll come and see you when she's ready," her aunt said. It was the most comfort that Deb's voice had ever brought her. When she saw the relief in Leo's eyes, she continued. "She's safe now. Marion has her at home; already checked her out here. They've been swarmed with police all day. We found her in the woods not too far from you," she said. "Looked like she tried to go get help for the two of you but couldn't make it."

Leo's chest tightened. "She's okay," she said. Sebago yawned and licked her paw as if this were just any other Saturday in September.

"She's okay." Mike placed a hand on Deb's shoulder. Deb looked to Leo for permission, and Leo assented with a slight nod. She touched Leo's ankle from above the covers of the clinic bed. It was a sweet, maternal gesture that was oddly welcome. "And you are, too," Deb said.

>>>>>> <<<<<<

Later, Leo heard a knock at her aunt and uncle's door. Sebbie rose to her paws and stood alert. Leo had to walk slowly to the door, clutching her side gingerly.

Tate Mulder stood on the other side, beautiful as ever. The brisk air played with her dark curls, and her golden-brown eyes reflected the light of the day. It was no longer raining. She was smiling. "Hi."

"Hi," Leo said and returned the look.

Tate glanced behind her and pointed her thumb to the front yard. "Can we talk?"

"Yeah." They started out to the grass, and Leo was just about to shut the door behind her when Sebbie poked her nose through. "Alright, you can come," Leo whispered. "But no funny business, ma'am." Sebago huffed and trotted out ahead of them.

Leo and Tate sat in the yard together, much like Leo had been doing that very first day in the summer when Tate had appeared in her driveway uninvited. It was quiet for a few moments, then Tate finally spoke up. "I don't remember much," she admitted. She didn't meet Leo's eyes.

"I figured you wouldn't," Leo said. "I wish I didn't."

Then she thought about that statement again. "Actually, no, I'm glad I remember."

That got Tate's attention. "You are? Wasn't it scary being down there looking for me?"

"The not-knowing is much scarier." She may never tell Tate exactly what she went through to find her in the depths of the black hole in the woods beyond Eston's cemetery, but she would not forget. Not again, if she could help it.

Tate nodded slowly. She eyed Sebago as the dog chewed a toy a few paces away. "I guess I was right about some things, huh?" she chuckled.

"You were." Leo picked a few blades of grass from the ground. "Listen, ah—" she began. "I've decided to go to college next year. Community college, anyway. They have a really pretty campus out by the ocean in Portland."

Tate froze for a moment, then smiled. "We can leave Eston now," she said.

"I think we can. The black hole is gone. Like it was never there in the first place." Leo shrugged and leaned back. "I dunno. I feel . . . lighter, somehow. Before, leaving wasn't even a possibility in my head. I thought I would be here forever. But I'm excited to go somewhere new."

"I'm happy for you," Tate said. "Truly. I've been thinking of doing the same. Maybe head to New York after all." It was quiet between them again. She adjusted the hem of her shirt, cleared her throat before she could speak. "You know I love you."

"I do." Leo could guess where this was going, and it did not scare her.

"I'm sorry." She shifted her weight. "It would be much better for both of us if we moved on, I think," Tate said after a deep, shaky breath.

Not trusting herself to talk just yet, Leo nodded. It was not fear nor anger that filled her gut, but a bittersweet kind of ache. They were two parallel universes in constant orbit; obsessive reflections of each other growing closer and closer with each mesmerized revolution. Their inevitable collision had left calamity in its wake. A supermassive black hole. She loosened her grip on the grass. "It would be," she agreed. She saw a glimmer in Tate's eyes and felt a stab through her heart. "I'm sorry, too. I was cruel."

"I was selfish."

The words were a tender catharsis. She cleared her throat after a moment. "It's okay. The vast majority of young adult relationships end a lot messier than ours is ending." Leo nudged her playfully and bit back her own pain.

Tate laughed, but it came out more like a hiccup. "Well, the vast majority of relationships don't have to deal with cryptids and liminal spaces, or towns that don't let you leave. Their problems are, like, flirting with another girl or something. They don't have to contend with weird shit."

"Sounds boring." Leo sniffled.

She smirked. "There's not much more I can think to say. But I'm happy that I had you for a while. And I'm happy that you're leaving. Neither of us belong here anymore."

The two girls sat on the grass for a while longer until the breeze grew too harsh for their liking, and Sebago scratched at the front door to be let back inside. They stood up to part ways but hesitated. Tate was half-turned to head up the driveway but looked at Leo with something that seemed like wonder.

Leo was tired of crying today. She took a step forward and held Tate's face ever so gently, watching for any sign of protest. When she saw none, she planted a soft kiss on her lips and lingered there for a few beats, electricity flying everywhere they touched. Crows chirped a ways away, a trio of them chattering amongst themselves. A murder that was somehow a comforting sight.

Finally, Tate stepped back. "Bye, Leo," she said. She rubbed her crooked nose and walked backward up the driveway in the direction of her house, hands stuffed in her pockets.

"Bye, Tate." Leo stepped back, too, joining Sebago on the small porch of her aunt and uncle's house, and watched as Tate turned up the road. The three crows in her yard continued their warbling, and then fell silent, staring in unison as the girl was lost beyond the trees.

ACKNOWLEDGEMENTS

I have poured a lot of things into this book over the last few years. It's nothing special, nothing groundbreaking in the horror genre. And it wasn't meant to be. *Let the Woods Keep Our Bodies* is an amalgamation of my time spent in college in Boston, studying abroad in London, living long-term somewhere other than my hometown in Maine for the first time, and all the stories I loved (and continue to love) during that time of my life. It's a love letter to all the great queer horror writers who have come before me (of which there are too many to name). It is a quiet sort of small-town story that could happen anywhere, anytime. It could be happening now. It will happen again.

That being said, I don't think this book could have been published by anyone other than Max Booth III and Lori Michelle of Ghoulish Books. Thank you for your patience, guidance, and feedback throughout this process. I doubt Leo and Tate would have ever seen the light of day had Ghoulish not opened its doors for unsolicited manuscript submissions in the spring of 2022, and I count myself among the extremely lucky to be working with you, especially as a debut author. Thank you for taking a chance on me.

Thanks to Ryan Caskey for the amazing cover art.

Thanks to Anna Lowy and Jamie Clark, my college roommate and classmate, respectively. You each read drafts and pieces of this book while it was still an absolute mess of half-formed ideas that I was afraid to share with anyone other than those who were in my same field of study (because then at least you would *get it*)—thank you for taking the time to do so.

Thanks to Mum and Dad, for encouraging me along the way and giving me a safe space to be authentically myself.

Thanks to my sibling for being my best friend.

And thank you, reader, for sticking around this long. It's been nice spending time with you. Perhaps we'll meet again soon.

ABOUT THE AUTHOR

Ellie (E. M.) Roy (she/they) is a writer and lover of all things weird, horrific, and dark, especially that which contains broader implications about society and the queer experience. After obtaining a B.A. in English from Boston University and graduating straight into a worldwide pandemic in 2020, her shorter work has appeared in a small handful of publications. She lives just outside of Portland, Maine with their parents, sibling, and dog, Boo. *Let the Woods Keep Our Bodies* (Ghoulish Books, 2023) is their debut novel.

SPOOKY TALES FROM GHOULISH BOOKS 2023

LIKE REAL | Shelly Lyons
ISBN: 978-1-943720-82-8 $16.95

This mind-bending body horror rom-com is a rollicking Cronenbergian gene splice of *Idle Hands* and *How to Lose a Guy in 10 Days*. It's freaky. It's fun. It's LIKE REAL.

XCRMNTMNTN | Andrew Hilbert
ISBN: 978-1-943720-81-1 $14.95

When a pile of shit from space lands near a renowned filmmaker's set, inspiration strikes. Take a journey up a cosmic mountain of excrement with the director and his film crew as they ascend into madness led only by their own vanity and obsession. This is a nightmare about creation. This is a dream about poop. This is a call to arms against vowels. This is *XCRMNTMNTN*.

BOUND IN FLESH | edited by Lor Gislason
ISBN: 978-1-943720-83-5 $16.95

Bound in Flesh: An Anthology of Trans Body Horror brings together 13 trans and non-binary writers, using horror to both explore the darkest depths of the genre and the boundaries of flesh. A disgusting good time for all! Featuring stories by Hailey Piper, Joe Koch, Bitter Karella, and others.

CONJURING THE WITCH | Jessica Leonard
ISBN: 978-1-943720-84-2 $16.95

Conjuring the Witch is a dark, haunted story about what those in power are willing to do to stay in power, and the sins we convince ourselves are forgivable.

WHAT HAPPENED WAS IMPOSSIBLE |
E. F. Schraeder
ISBN: 978-1-943720-85-9 $14.95

Everyone knows the woman who escapes a massacre is a final girl, but who is the final boy? *What Happened Was Impossible* follows the life of Ida Wright, a man who knows how to capitalize on his childhood tragedies . . . even when he caused them.

THE ONLY SAFE PLACE LEFT IS THE DARK|
Warren Wagner

ISBN: 978-1-943720-86-6 $14.95

In *The Only Safe Place Left is the Dark*, an HIV positive gay man must leave the relative safety of his cabin in the woods to brave the zombie apocalypse and find the medication he needs to stay alive.

THE SCREAMING CHILD| Scott Adlerberg

ISBN: 978-1-943720-87-3 $16.95

Scott Adlerberg's *The Screaming Child* is a mystery horror novel told by a grieving woman working on a book about an explorer who was murdered in a remote wilderness region, only to get caught up in a dangerous journey after hearing the distant screams from her own vanished child somewhere in the woods.

RAINBOW FILTH | Tim Meyer

ISBN: 978-1-943720-88-0 $14.95

Rainbow Filth is a weirdo horror novella about a small cult that believes a rare psychedelic substance can physically transport them to another universe.

LET THE WOODS KEEP OUR BODIES| E. M. Roy

ISBN: 978-1-943720-89-7 $16.95

The familiar becomes strange the longer you look at it. Leo Bates navigates a broken sense of reality, shattered memories, and a distrust of herself in order to find her girlfriend Tate and restore balance to their hometown of Eston—if such a thing ever existed to begin with.

SAINT GRIT| Kayli Scholz

ISBN: 978-1-943720-90-3 $14.95

One brooding summer, Nadine Boone pricks herself on a poisonous manchineel tree in the Florida backcountry. Upon self-orgasm, Nadine conjures a witch that she calls Saint Grit. Pitched as *Gummo* meets *The Craft*, Saint Grit grows inside of Nadine over three decades, wreaking repulsive havoc on a suspicious cast of characters in a small town known as Sugar Bends. Comes in Censored or Uncensored cover.

Ghoulish Books
PO Box 1104
Cibolo, TX 78108

☐ LIKE REAL   16.95

☐ XCRMNTMNTN   14.95

☐ BOUND IN FLESH   16.95

☐ CONJURING THE WITCH   16.95

☐ WHAT HAPPENED WAS IMPOSSIBLE   14.95

☐ THE ONLY SAFE PLACE LEFT IS THE DARK   14.95

☐ THE SCREAMING CHILD   16.95

☐ RAINBOW FILTH   14.95

☐ LET THE WOODS KEEP OUR BODIES   16.95

☐ SAINT GRIT   14.95
    Censored | Uncensored

Ship to:

Name   _____

Address _____

City_____State_____Zip_____

Phone Number   _____

                Book Total: $_____

          Shipping Total: $_____

           Grand Total: $_____

Not all titles available for immediate shipping. All credit card purchases must be made online at GhoulishBooks.com. Shipping is 5.80 for one book and an additional dollar for each additional book. Contact us for international shipping prices. All checks and money orders should be made payable to Perpetual Motion Machine.

Patreon:
www.patreon.com/pmmpublishing

Website:
www.GhoulishBooks.com

Facebook:
www.facebook.com/GhoulishBooks

Twitter:
@GhoulishBooks

Instagram:
@GhoulishBookstore

Newsletter:
www.PMMPNews.com

Linktree:
linktr.ee/ghoulishbooks

Printed in the USA
CPSIA information can be obtained
at www.ICGtesting.com
JSHW031206280823
47305JS00005B/13